What the
Other Three
Don't Know

OTHER BOOKS BY SPENCER HYDE

Waiting for Fitz

What the Other Three Don't Know

A NOVEL BY
SPENCER HYDE

SHADOW
MOUNTAIN

This is a work of fiction. Characters and events in this book are products of the author's imagination or are represented fictitiously.

Visit us at shadowmountain.com

Library of Congress Cataloging-in-Publication Data

Names: Hyde, Spencer, author.
Title: What the other three don't know : a novel / by Spencer Hyde.
Other titles: What the other three do not know
Description: Salt Lake City : Shadow Mountain, [2020] | Audience: Ages 14. | Audience: Grades 10–12. | Summary: When a loner, a jock, an outsider, and an Internet influencer go river rafting together for a school assignment, the four strangers end up sharing their secrets and relying on each other when the trip turns dangerous.
Identifiers: LCCN 2019038747 | ISBN 9781629727325 (hardcover)
Subjects: CYAC: Rafting (Sports)—Fiction. | Secrets—Fiction. | Survival—Fiction. | Friendship—Fiction. | Rivers—Fiction.
Classification: LCC PZ7.1.H917 Wh 2020 | DDC [Fic]—dc23
LC record available at https://lccn.loc.gov/2019038747

Printed in the United States of America
Lake Book Manufacturing, Inc., Melrose Park, IL

10   9   8   7   6   5   4   3   2   1

For Brittany, my bright star

"Stories of life are often more like rivers than books."

—NORMAN MACLEAN

ONE

My mother once told me that when a star implodes, it can shrink to the size of a wedding ring and still weigh two thousand trillion tons. That's what I thought about as I turned her wedding ring in my palm before dropping the necklace beneath my shirt. I felt the weight around my neck, the cold silver chain it hung on.

My dad left us ten years ago and is now commercial fishing somewhere off the coast of Alaska. My mother died two years ago rafting the Snake River, though her knowledge of physics didn't keep her from that sink.

Seventeen. Parentless. Ill-fated. No-win. Cursed. Call it what you want, they were gone, and I was still kicking rocks and living with Grandpa in a trailer the size of a nickel in a town the size of a postage stamp.

Tetonia, Idaho. Population: 300. Just outside the bustling town of Victor. Population: 2,000. Two of those people in Tetonia were an old man and his jaded granddaughter.

The old man was my grandfather, Aldo Lutz, the town mortician in Victor. I'm the granddaughter—Indiana "Indie" Lutz.

My parents named me Indiana because I was born on the road-side next to a weathered, warped green state sign that read *Now Leaving Indiana*. I'm sure they had no idea how prophetic that sign would be. Everyone left me.

At this point in my life, only a hero could save me, and I wasn't the hero type. I couldn't save myself from the dark thoughts, the quiet moments of guilt and loss, the manic shouting into the ether that everything had been taken from me. Wherever I went, something felt like it didn't belong. But more and more, that something was starting to have my name, my face, my life.

I leaned against the hearse parked in front of our trailer. We didn't live in a funeral home because with so few people in town, we only needed a small space for cremation or prepping bodies for viewing before they went into the ground. It wasn't necessary to have an entire house dedicated to the whole pageantry of death. Plus, the spectacle of grief was more than I could bear.

I wrote on the back window of the hearse with my finger, ghosting the words into the collected dust: *It's Not You (Yet). It's Me*. And then I walked around the side of the car and wrote something else on the passenger door: *Dead Inside*.

"Usually," said Grandpa as he stepped out of the trailer, pointing at my message. "Thankfully, Bury will be the only body in the back today." He patted Bury's head as the giant Bernese Mountain dog trotted alongside him.

I looked at our old trailer, the siding curling away in places, a drooping front porch, and the small windows reflecting light back onto the landscape. The trees towered over the trailer and rained leaves in the fall, so much so that we used the same shovel in the fall for the leaves as we did in the winter for the snow.

Some nights, I'd sit under the giant ash trees and watch the stars throw themselves in bright arcs and fizzle out into black. I used to stargaze with Mom. She would tell me how we were just a tiny speck on a giant map of billions and billions of galaxies, each one filled with those little burning lamps overhead. She said that Aristotle talked about the stars like they were just a grouping of crystal spheres on some crankshaft.

I shouldered my duffel bag in what was a surprisingly cold summer morning. It had been a heavy-clouded winter and a no-clouded summer. The branches of the aspens swayed in a morning breeze. The sun emerged, throwing long shadows in front of Grandpa's rattletrap truck. I wished we were taking the truck instead of the hearse, but the hearse was better for long drives. As if there weren't enough rumors about the old mortician and his granddaughter.

Grandpa walked to the car and yelled at me to get in. I stared back at our little stamp of earth we called home as the hearse rose over a ridge and dipped past other homesteads. Bury nuzzled my arm before situating himself in the back seat.

We drove through the spanning shadows of the Teton mountain range. The French called the range *Les Trois Tetons*, or "The Three Breasts." Typical French. The range had already shed most of its snowpack under the summer sun. The white walls of the aspens towered over the roads, their arms touching, a tunnel of green and white, with red-naped sapsuckers pecking at the bark.

I wondered if I'd packed correctly for the river trip. Five

days on the water in Hells Canyon. An eight-hour drive to the drop-in point.

I was on my way to meet up with three other students from Mrs. Wixom's journalism course. Only seniors were allowed to take the course, and in order to enroll, you had to go on what she called "The Summer Scoop." Dumb name, but Wixom was the coolest teacher at Teton High School, so we did what she said.

There were four groups this year, each with four or five students. One group was on horseback in Jackson, one group was rock climbing in the Wind River Range, one group was fly-fishing near Henry's Fork on the Snake River. Our group was running the river in Hells Canyon. All groups were camping.

Mrs. Wixom said she wanted each person to write a human-interest story about one other person on the trip. "Experiential learning is how you bond," she'd said. "It'll make for a strong class for the entire senior year."

Whatever. I wasn't about to write a human-interest story.

My plan was to write about the commercialization of the outdoors and how it was ruining the wild. I wanted to become a journalist in order to reveal the truth of the world to people— that it's cold, that people don't care, that you'll find yourself half-way down the rabbit hole before realizing you'll never see the light of day again. Take the pills. Drink the potion. Walk into a world that's just as lost as this one. That's what I wanted people to know. That was the truth as I saw it.

I had been interested in all-things-journalism since my freshman year, after I won an award from our mayor for my lo-cal reporting on the water levels of the dam and how they affect fly-fishing during our busiest tourist months. Dad loved to fly-fish, so I wrote it thinking I could send it to him as some last effort at connecting or something. Did it work? No, but that's how it started.

I asked Mrs. Wixom if I could do a sequel to that piece and go with the fly-fishing group—I wanted to spend days on the river, full of sky and flies and the slow eddies where the fish wait patiently for their next bite—but she said the groups were assigned at random and we had no say in the matter. Well, at least I thought it was random until I got the rest of the story from the others.

I checked on Bury, who was on his back, belly up and legs splayed, covering the entirety of the back seat. I was glad Grandpa allowed him to get in the car with us. I have trouble saying no when it comes to rescuing animals, and Bury was the sweetest thing I'd ever seen. I'd picked him up six months earlier from the vet in Victor, half his face rubbed off because some negligent driver had been too drunk to remember his dog was tied to the tailgate. Even if Bury took up a lot of space, it was space that needed filling.

I kind of felt like Bury at times—taking up too much space, unwelcome except by a select few people, and always in need of help from others, my past a wash. A rescue dog, but with less hair and more freckles. I hated that. I wanted to be on my own and earn my own keep and not rely on anybody, not even Grandpa and his stoic ways.

If I were to describe myself, I would say that I was intelligent and ambitious, but also overly—and overtly—cynical as a way of pushing others away. I spend most of my time reading books or fly-fishing, even if the weather is frigid, because it makes me feel closer to my parents. I'm barely five feet tall with hair just curly enough that it tries my patience most mornings. I keep it pulled back at all times. Oh, and I'm a pessimist with way too many freckles. My face is like a connect-the-dots of all eighty-eight constellations.

And perhaps I'm too focused on what's coming next instead of what's happening in the moment, but I can't help rolling my eyes at the clichés hanging in the halls of my school: *Live in the moment. Seize the day. If you don't risk anything, you risk everything.*

Maybe I needed to risk more. I hadn't had anything published since that dam article three years previous, though not for lack of trying. I'd written an article on the minimum wage in small towns after working as an assistant to a big-game vet, calving in the fields for two months. I'd also worked as a vending-machine stocker in Driggs and written about the energy suck those machines are, and I'd waited tables in Jackson to study the way tourism bolsters the economy at the expense of the land. No hits. No interest.

I was now technically a senior and needed one more big publication. Something that could go viral. All I wanted to do was publish a journalism piece that garnered national attention, earned me an academic scholarship, and offered me an escape from the small-town claustrophobia I felt in Tetonia. I was tired of living in a nothing place and having nobody. I needed out. That's what I wanted. Out of this gorgeous hole. Sure, I could be mad all day about being in the place, but the beauty of it was too much to handle sometimes.

Those who have not grown up in the West might not understand how the world looks like it can go on forever, like the blue sky will never end. They wouldn't understand the grand feeling of those mountains and the unimaginable vistas that have become a normal, everyday sight for most in my town. Perhaps that was one of the oddest parts about living in a beautiful place: beauty became common, even boring; expected, even ignored.

Despite its beauty, sometimes it seemed that Tetonia wanted to remind me that I couldn't leave. It was almost like memories and fears and loss and grief were aligned with the physical borders of our little town. Like, if I could just cross into a new place, new geography, I might feel lighter. I might feel less beholden to some pressure pushing inward. Like, maybe memories made in the town weren't really mine. Maybe those many years in Tetonia belonged to somebody else.

And those who have not grown up in a trailer without their parents might not understand how the world also feels like everything is underwater, and that you'll never have enough guts or energy or optimism or downright strength to kick your way to the surface. I'm not growing gills over here, though I've been trying for years. I have this dream that Aquaman will swoop in and pick me up at some point, but my sea legs are lost in the trailer and I'm tired of looking for them.

We'd made good time on our trip, because Grandpa had insisted on leaving at six in the morning, even though I didn't believe that anything in the world even existed at that hour. I imagined the earth as some kind of Minecraft map, putting itself together each morning before I woke, one pixelated block at a time. But how could anything be in place by six a.m.? I figured it must be nothing but a blank map and some shovels resting against the dark void. It made me think of how kids play hide-and-seek—if they cover their eyes, no one can find them. Life stops. The windows darken. The doors lock.

I started to doze off, and when Grandpa nudged me, I kept my eyes closed.

"You were moving slow as the government this morning, Indie."

A few response options presented themselves, their sole purpose to provide *otherness*, or choice, right?

1. *Tell him I was awake and listening, then fade back into my dream world where Aquaman rescues me with his shirt* off *and his wit* on.
2. *Mention I have a flesh-eating bacteria and cut off my hand as proof, thus forcing him to drive me to the hospital instead of making me go on the river trip.*
3. *Roll out of the car and escape to camp in the mountains by myself.*
4. *Answer him, step up to the past, and face the day like I should.*

After Mom died, I started seeing options present themselves before my face as if they were being projected right in front of me, like I could literally scroll through the available choices of how to respond or what to say. I think that maybe it happened because Mom's accident would never be on any list like that, and after she was gone I felt like I needed options, a way out. Maybe some large, saloon-style doors that opened into some other existence.

I chose response option number 4, of course. I opened my eyes to face the day. "The government is a well-oiled machine, Grandpa. You know that. Finest bunch of people in these United States."

"Government is nothing but crap where we should have apple butter."

We kept things light to keep from talking about the heavier stuff at our feet, the stuff we dragged around with us, the weightier matters that made us upset or even depressed. We didn't talk about those things. We made corny jokes and stupid puns or talked about odd phenomena or things I knew got Grandpa all flustered—like the government. Humor displaced grief. Anything to keep us from facing it.

With my head against the window, I watched as we passed the cemetery in Victor. It made me think of elephant graveyards and how, according to legend, older elephants wandered off from the group when they knew they were going to die. Maybe it was a myth, but the truth was just as interesting, if not more so. My science teacher, Mrs. Weyand, said that when an elephant dies, other elephants wait around and pick up their friend's or family member's bones and walk around with them for a while before moving on.

I often wondered if elephants said anything to the bones of the dead. I liked to imagine them softly touching the skulls of their lost brother or sister or mother and whispering things to them in their own language.

Mrs. Weyand also said that when elephants walk past places they have lost loved ones, they stop for a few minutes, silently. I'm inclined to believe her. But I didn't realize that the entire town visiting Mom's gravesite was nothing more than a herd of elephants. A bunch of elephants in a small town in Idaho. A zoo of grief.

Years ago, Grandpa promised my mom—Joyce—that he'd watch out for me if anything ever happened to her. At the time, she brushed it aside. "We have our own place in Victor, and we're doing just fine, Dad," she'd said. She taught physics at Teton High School, so everybody knew my mom and how she was the greatest. Way better than me. Example: I was known as *Joyce's daughter*. She wasn't known as *Indie's mom*. Then things got real.

I mean, we all end up as ash anyway, right? Body to ash, heat moving from one thing to another. That's what Newton was on about, right? The friction. The heat. The way energy moves and flows like a river.

I nudged Bury, and he nuzzled my arm again, so I took his snout and pretended I was shifting gears. One—three—six. I hummed like a race car as I moved his nose around. I felt the shape of his skull, the way his ears dipped and turned, and the way he yawned and softly growled before licking my hand and rolling away. I wiped my hand on my ratty jeans.

"Did I forget anything, Bury?" I said, eyeing my go-bag.

I'd only be on the river for five days, so I didn't want to overpack. I'd made sure I had some crossword puzzles in my bag and something to write with, as well as my fly-rod—because Grandpa taught me that fly-fishing is the only way to experience eternity, and he was right.

A mountain bluebird lighted on an aspen branch and blurred as the car cruised past. Options presented themselves—how

I might talk to Grandpa about where we were headed, how I might get out of what my therapist was calling "Exposure Therapy" and what Grandpa was calling a week of "Cowboy Up and Face It," but I didn't know what to choose or what to say.

Instead, I thought of my bed back home and the wood-burning stove radiating heat. I loved the distinct pops I'd hear in the middle of the night, a sappy knot exploding in the enclosed flames. Sometimes when I couldn't sleep, I would wander out to put more wood on the stove and see Grandpa asleep on the couch next to it, an old Louis L'Amour novel or a dog-eared fishing magazine resting on his chest. I'd often see piles of tightly tied flies—something Grandpa did to pass the time when he was tired. I'd sit next to him and borrow some of his blanket and snuggle with Bury and watch the flames flicker.

"Supposed to be pretty wet, being on the water and all," Grandpa said.

"What an astute observation."

"Just like your mother. Obnoxious as a braying donkey."

I worried about Grandpa more than he knew. He was my last anchor in the wall, and I was getting tired of climbing.

"Any other advice?" I asked.

"Nope."

I'd recently come to cherish the idea that I was living someone else's life, in someone else's skin, and that my true life was whole and healthy and filled with laughter and light and somewhere far away from this one. I didn't want to be a burden to Grandpa—he'd already raised his kids. He shouldn't have to do it again.

The car ticked in the morning cool. Grandpa hummed and

stared out into the valley, two shocks of white hair jutting out over his large ears, with nothing but baldness beneath the 1920s newsboy cap he insisted on wearing. His white push-broom mustache and his languid language gave him a country softness, but he'd knock you over soon as invite you to dinner. I knew that. But the world tilted differently around Aldo Lutz. He acted like the heavy stuff in life was just something caught in the wind, just passing by, and only the happy stuff stuck around and settled in.

Me? I was often tight, taut, like a fishing line snagged.

I hadn't asked Grandpa to make the eight-hour drive to Riggins, Idaho, where my fellow journalism students would set in late and raft for a short time on the Snake River before setting up our first camp. I told him he could stay home and I'd go on the school shuttle with the rest of my group—whoever they were—but he insisted. He kept saying he was helping me follow "doctor's orders." To tell you the truth, he was good people.

We passed old ranches with their rusty plowshares and tattered hackamores hanging from old rakes and knotty tree limbs. Giant tractors sighed in the distance, their turning and harvesting a sound beyond my reach. Cattle sat in the morning sunlight. We passed the angler shop, the farmers market, the Knotty Pine, the Victor Post, and the Grand Teton Brewery. We passed a herd of elk grazing and watched as giant birds tucked their wings and dipped into the fields for breakfast.

In the distance, I saw an osprey crouched in a tall aspen, light playing off her hunched feathers. Trucks were pulling drift boats toward water—off to fish, those boats. It was reaching the peak of fly-fishing season. Many of the fly-fishing guides would sell their soul to have the season be year-round.

Each town is like a river, currents fighting for the path. The water is always trying to change direction, to overflow, to run onto new ground. But some banks are too high. Some rivers move too fast. Some rivers dry up. And some rivers run because that's all they've ever done.

$$\approx$$

Four hours later, after a couple bathroom stops and more than one gas-station-snack run, we stopped by the river to let Bury stretch his unwieldy body. Grandpa leaned against the hearse, popped some sunflower seeds in his mouth, and began chewing. He'd been trying to cut back on tobacco and needed something to occupy his time and his mouth. Spoiler: it usually wasn't words.

"Well."

He said that sometimes, as if to state that everything was okay, or that life was moving along as he expected, or to let me know he was willing to talk, even if it was just to say one word.

"Wish I had my fishing pole," I said.

"It's called a rod. If you can't call it a rod, you shouldn't fish, and you shouldn't talk about fishing."

I let him know I was just teasing, but he didn't change his look.

"I don't know if I can do this, Grandpa," I said.

He looked at me and spit shells onto the ground. "Have you

forgotten everything, or are you just messing with an old man again? What do we say when we hook a fish?"

"Hand that rod to God."

"That's right. Hand that rod to God. Let that hookset work its magic." He put another handful of seeds in his mouth and shifted them into one side. "What do we say once we've got that thing on the line?"

"Let it run."

"And what does that mean?"

"I'm not a child, Grandpa. I remember."

"And what does that mean?"

He had this habit of repeating himself when I didn't offer the answer he was looking for, kind of like some of our teachers did at Teton High. It was annoying.

"You let the fish run before yanking the barb and reminding it that it cannot leave your line. You let it dive and roam as you slowly bring it in. You keep the rod up and let line out if you need to. You can't rush a big fish."

"You can't rush a big fish. Damn straight. If you let it run, you can keep it hooked all day until it's so tired it has no choice but to give in to your will."

"Right."

"The catch is fun. But you have to remember the release."

I kicked rocks at my feet and whistled to Bury. He turned his massive head toward me, and I tossed a stick his way. He sniffed it and rolled it with his nose and then sauntered closer to the water for a drink.

"That's the easiest part."

"That's the hardest part," he said.

"What do you mean?"

"You know what I mean. If you don't, you don't. I think you'll learn it soon enough."

Grandpa always seemed to leave out too much, and he didn't bother feeling bad about leaving so many questions floating around. He was able to suspend multiple things in the air, not worrying where they might fall or about which one to catch first. But he knew I was smart enough to get it, eventually. I wasn't so sure, but he seemed to think I'd find a way.

"Let's get you to the canyon. Call that mammoth of yours to the car."

The next four hours passed in relative silence. I worked on crosswords—Will Shortz, the *New York Times* crossword puzzle master, was my hero and secret crush—and Grandpa put on some Johnny Cash and kept singing "How high is the water, Momma?"

When we finally arrived, I was ready to go back to sleep or turn around or take off into the trees with Bury and never return.

Why had I agreed to this? I'd been asking myself that for weeks leading up to the Summer Scoop trip. But now it was here and so was I. What was I supposed to do—turn my back on the river that knew more about me than most people?

Grandpa killed the ignition, and I stared at the Hells Whitewater Tours van parked fifty yards away.

"Why am I doing this?"

"Because you're like your mother."

"I guess."

"It's time you did as the doctor ordered and faced the river. I can't do it for you. Nobody can."

I looked out the window as a bird tipped from the top of a tree and dove into tall grass. Spotted a late lunch, no doubt.

"You also said this was your way of getting out of Tetonia for a while, as I recall. You said this trip might provide you with an article that would punch you a ticket elsewhere."

"Can you still come with me—wherever I end up?" I asked.

"We've got a year to decide. But, yes, that's the beauty of our home. It's mobile."

"You're worse than Mom," I said.

"Bad jokes become us. Don't forget your roots."

The school shuttle had already arrived and now crawled out of the parking lot, leaving three of my classmates in a puff of exhaust. I recognized them, but I didn't get out of the car. That would give the journey an actual beginning, and I wasn't ready.

"Do you think she'll be there?" I asked quietly. "I mean, do you think she'll be with me? Whatever. It's a stupid question."

"There are lots of stupid questions, but that's not one of them."

I leaned over and hugged Grandpa, then kissed Bury on the mouth and wiped away the slobber from his massive tongue pancaking my face.

"See you two in a week."

I sighed, got out, and closed the car door, my duffel bag at my feet. I waved to Grandpa. Bury's giant face fogged up the window, reanimating the words *Dead Inside*. I felt that way, like grief had cored me and run away with the pit. Leaving Bury and

Grandpa was something I hadn't done since Mom died. It felt impossible.

I wondered what other impossible things I would face. I had to be at least half-mad to run the same stretch of river that took my mother. I wondered why I was willing to go on this trip.

I wondered what it would take to save me.

I wished I could stay home and take Bury on a walk and watch my favorite show. But it was time to face the curse, to face the river, to face my past. And I needed a story. The river was running a path through my mind, through my life, and I needed to start risking things again.

I sat on my duffel fifty yards from the others, waiting to see if they'd leave without me. I wondered if they'd notice me. I didn't want to walk over to them. If I didn't move from that spot, maybe Grandpa would turn around and realize he was asking too much of me, that my doctor was asking too much of me.

I opened my crossword book and looked at 34 down: a four-letter word for "friend." I felt my guts sink. I didn't have any of those in my life. The trees cut up the sunlight and threw laddered shadows onto the asphalt in front of me. Maybe I would find something beyond a partial friend—something lasting, something stable.

I wrote "mate" for 34 down. But it felt wrong. How was I to know I should have filled in the empty spaces with *Skye, Wyatt,* and *Shelby?*

TWO

snatched a penny off the ground and turned it over and over in my fingers. Mom sometimes talked at home about the first law of probability—that one chance event has no effect on the next chance event and its result.

But what were the odds that this particular coin would end up at my feet on this particular day? That coin had been traveling my way for seventeen years, and I was about to flip it, and it was going to give me either heads or tails. I'd had far too many tails in my life, I decided, so I wedged the edge of the coin in a gap in the cracked asphalt and decided that if it was going to fall, it wasn't going to be my hand that pushed it one way or the other. But God has a sense of humor, and as I stood up and started toward the van, the coin fell.

Heads or tails? I couldn't say.

What I could say: not much. I didn't have word one for the motley group of people standing in front of me at the guide station in Riggins, Idaho.

A tall, lean boy rested against the van, holding a climbing rope and tying knots in it. Untying. Tying. His face was bright and craggy, covered in seams from the sun, like the crimps on a climbing route. His cheeks sunk into dimples, and he watched me from the corner of his eye. He had curly, oak-colored hair, and skin the color of the light-brown rocks in Moab and Arches. I knew him by reputation. Skye Ellis was big news—a star athlete, scholarships, the works—but I hadn't seen him in over a year. Nobody had. And I didn't really care to see anybody in that moment.

"So, what's up with you?" he said.

I didn't know how to respond. I dropped my duffel next to the Hells Whitewater Tours van Mrs. Wixom had listed in the itinerary and adjusted my ponytail. Light spilled onto his face, and his black eyes reflected the afternoon sun.

I had some options of things I could tell him:

1. *Existential dread. What is life but question after question? Why even try?*
2. *Early onset bunions.*
3. *The dry cleaners keep starching my shirts, even though I tell them not to.*
4. *I'm judgmental as a defense mechanism, because I'm insecure.*
5. *I don't let people close to me for fear they will hurt me, and I've already dealt with that kind of thing enough for the rest of my life.*
6. *I ate brussels sprouts as a kid.*
7. *A lot.*

I didn't go with any of those options.

"Nothing," I said.

"We all have something," he said, pointing to his metal prosthetic leg.

I was surprised I hadn't noticed it right away, but brushed it aside, reminding myself I had other things to worry about.

"I guess," I said.

"Right. That's what they both said as well."

He pointed to where Wyatt Isom sat on a rock, sharpening a large blade. Wyatt had long, dirty-blond hair in a bun and a full face of soft features. He had on cargo shorts and a shirt that said "I'm a Prepper" with a World War I–style gas mask printed on it.

Beyond Wyatt was a girl adjusting her hair in the afternoon light, standing in front of an alder and talking to her phone. I didn't know her, but I knew *of* her. Shelby Trumane rolled with the popular girls and always seemed to be too busy for anybody or anything. She had a big mouth and beautiful features. She had one of those ridiculous selfie sticks and kept pausing, repositioning, and rerecording some spiel about something I couldn't quite hear. Whatever it was, it sounded like she was annoyed.

Spoiler: she spoke with the status quo tone of her group—*annoyed*.

"I'm guessing you're in Wixom's class?" I said to her.

"Obviously. Our driver ran into the bathroom. We're just waiting on him. And you. Last one here, and all," said Shelby.

"Sorry for the inconvenience."

"I don't mind waiting for beautiful things," Skye said, lifting my duffel into the van.

"You're pretty forward."

"Better than backward," he said.

I couldn't stop the heat or the red that rose to my face when he said "beautiful." I wasn't used to hearing that word applied to me. Maybe when talking to Grandpa about the scales on a fish or the way a horse's muscles flex during a full sprint or the way the Teton Mountains go purple in the right light. Maybe when shopping or admiring a painting in the Trailside Gallery in Jackson with Mom. Maybe then I could understand the word *beautiful*. But not when it was said about me.

I didn't know how to respond, so I decided to call him out on his language. "*Things?*"

"Sorry," he said. "People."

"I'm not people. I'm Indie."

"I'm Skye, with an *e*," he said, touching his prosthetic leg.

"Hi, Skye with an e."

"I know who you are," he said.

"And I know who you are. But do either of us really know one another?"

"Sure," he said.

"It's a small school, but that doesn't mean we know much beyond what we've heard. Where have you been, anyway?"

"Right. It doesn't matter."

"What?" I said.

"The *e* thing. I don't know why I said that."

His voice was deep, like it belonged in one of those old movies set in wartime where masses of people gathered around the radio to hear the news of the latest bombing raids or advances at the front.

"Because it does matter. Spelling matters. One letter matters.

It's the difference between 'hell' and 'hello.' Between 'slaughter' and 'laughter.' And as for the beautiful thing, you must mean her."

I pointed at Shelby, who put her phone in her pocket and then telescoped the selfie stick into a tiny rod that she slipped into her backpack.

"What?" she said, stepping next to us by the van.

"He said you're beautiful," I said.

Skye gave me the "Really?" look.

"Thanks, Skye." She smiled as if everyone told her she was beautiful. "I'm Shelby," she said at me. Not *to* me, because she had pulled her phone out again and was scrolling through it.

"Thanks for that," Skye said to me. "I bet she needs more material for her Insta Story on eating gluten free or whatever it is she's recording."

"I'm building a social media following," she said, without looking up from her phone.

I turned to Skye. "Weren't you, like, the star soccer player? What happened?"

"Where have you been?" said Shelby. "He lost his leg in a car accident over a year ago. The entire school knows."

"Apparently not," I said. "As I am part of the entirety and I didn't know."

I already hated Shelby. And Skye was annoyingly forward, even if he was complimentary. They both acted like they were used to people waiting for them and tending to their every need, so I decided to make them work for it. I wasn't at that river for them, anyway.

"I'll tell you the whole story on the river," he said. "Short version is that I was homeschooled this last year. Took some time to recover and learn how to use this stupid new leg."

He seemed pretty nonchalant about it, which surprised me. I didn't respond, as part of my new plan to avoid conversation and move on to the river without worrying about the extra baggage, or people, or anything really.

Our driver walked out of the station and adjusted his sunglasses. He had on Chacos, cargo shorts, and a Petzl tank top. An American flag bandana was tied around his neck.

"You must be Indiana," he said.

"Indie."

He checked his clipboard.

"That's all of us. Let's load up the van and get moving. The guide will be waiting at the drop-in point."

"You're not the guide?" I said.

"Nope, I'm just the driver. I won't be guiding until I pass training. This is my first summer rafting or doing much of anything outdoorsy really," he said. "The company opened up a year ago and was willing to take a chance on me."

"Where are you from?" said Skye.

"I'm visiting from Washington State University for a few months. Studying engineering, but I wanted to try this out. I'll be helping Sawyer with camp setup and the resupply on day three. We'll see you on the water soon enough."

Wyatt sheathed his knife and walked to the van, nodding at me as he threw his duffel into the back. The bag was covered in odd insignias and patches that read "Black Ops Zombie Recon" and "Zombie Outbreak Response Team" with the biohazard logo everywhere.

Wyatt's trailer was just a stone's throw from ours, so even if he was too cool to talk to me, he had to acknowledge that we were practically neighbors. Since we lived so close to one another, it meant that I knew his father was an abusive drunk and didn't appreciate Wyatt or his artistic talent. I'm not talking small-time sketches. I'm talking "worthy of Jackson Hole art gallery" work. Like, the big leagues. I'd seen his skill one afternoon when I was walking Bury and saw Wyatt painting a dilapidated barn in Tetonia.

I suddenly missed shopping with Mom in Jackson. I missed our visits to the art galleries. I knew we could never afford the paintings or bronzes in those places, but we could afford the hot chocolate and the drive from Victor over the Teton Pass. We could afford time together.

Wyatt claimed a seat in the van and stared out his window, tapping his foot against the floor, like a piston driving into the carpet.

"Just the four of us, I guess," said Skye as he hopped into the van and buckled in. "I didn't want to be with this group. No offense."

"Neither did I," said Shelby.

"Sorry you didn't get to pick another group. Couldn't your parents sign you up for some dressage camp in Jackson?" said Wyatt.

"You're right," Shelby said, feigning shock and putting her right hand to her chest in a mock-elegant way. "Why am I not at home riding my $100,000 horses? Dear me, they must be absolutely lost without Mumsy! Driver, I seem to have stepped into this crap-box of a car without my gloves!"

I couldn't help but laugh, even if that meant kind of aligning myself with Wyatt without even thinking about it. I noticed I felt defensive on his behalf, but wasn't sure why. It had to be geography, right? Because we were neighbors? What else could it be?

"Just saying. Don't complain when you can pay to have whatever you want," said Wyatt. "I bet your parents would buy you the river if you asked."

"That's not fair, man," said Skye.

"No, it's okay," said Shelby. "He's just jealous I get to wear fancy hats to expensive events and that I can, like, buy happiness if I want to. Maybe I will ask for the river as a birthday present. Maybe the whole state of Idaho."

Sitting behind her, Wyatt only saw the back of her head, but from my angle, I could see Shelby's eyes harden, her mouth a rigid line. Her neck flushed a light red, and her cheeks were booming with color.

"What about you, Indie?" said Skye.

"I'm just here for the free T-shirt."

"Right," said Skye.

"I'm serious. Hopefully it has some awesome pun about Hells Canyon and being in hell and all that, right? That's all I want. Hopefully it's sweat-wicking."

Skye shook his head. "Okay, if nobody is going to be honest, I'll start: My parents met with Wixom and said that I was ready for the river, that it would be a good challenge for me and they wanted to push me. I wanted to fly-fish. But whatever. I guess I don't mind rafting."

"Can you still do stuff with the new getup?" said Wyatt.

"More than you think," said Skye, shifting his leg.

"Alright," our driver said, climbing behind the wheel and cutting off our conversation. "Let's get you guys to Hells Canyon."

Our driver—who had clearly read through the brochure—spent the next half hour telling us about Hells Canyon and the river, how it was the deepest river gorge in North America, how artifacts from old mining camps and prehistoric tribes dotted the land, how the river carved through more than 200,000 acres of wilderness, rimrocks, and the Seven Devils Mountain Range—Ogre, She Devil, He Devil, Twin Imps, Devil's Throne, Mt. Belial, and Goblin. Wyatt perked up when these peaks were listed.

I felt anxiety coursing through me, aware that I would be confronting not only whitewater rapids but the Snake River itself, where the Hells Canyon Recreational Area split in two and would take us back toward Tetonia and Victor.

I wasn't listening to the driver detail the petroglyphs we'd see or how underwater volcanoes shaped the rocks in the canyon, or the fact that the river was a mile below the land and more than a hundred feet deep in places, or that there were at least two sections of class IV rapids.

I wasn't listening to any of that. I was only thinking about the weight of the ring around my neck and the many hours over the past year when I'd sat on the banks of the Snake River near Victor and thought about Mom with a sweet taste in my mouth and a bitter feeling in my heart. I'd watch fly-fishing guides in their drift boats and think about how Dad used to take me drifting on the Snake, and then my whole day would be spent trying to come up for air.

I was haunted by water, by how beautiful it was and how calming it looked. How it was able to curl through anything and stay blue, sink anything but stay moving, carve through a life and take the whole world with it.

Our driver said we were ten minutes from the site. We continued through tons of massive trees, and while I stared out the window, I heard Wyatt whispering, "Monkshood. Elephant head. Snapdragon. Ponderosa pine. Red alder. Western larch."

"What?" I said.

"Nothing. Just looking at the trees."

I watched a large osprey dive into the fading afternoon light, just beyond the trees Wyatt was listing.

"Can we all agree not to write about each other?" said Skye.

"Wixom said we had to write about each other," said Shelby. "That was the whole point." She stabbed at her phone with her finger. "Are you kidding me? I don't have any service."

Wyatt laughed.

"Shut up, Wyatt," said Shelby.

"It must be tough to know you won't be the first to like something. All those little hearts, and no red to fill them in. Who is going to do it all? Sigh."

"You just said 'Sigh' out loud, you know that, right?" said Shelby. "Everybody hear that?"

"In fact, something might go viral over the next few days and you'll be the last one to know about it," said Wyatt. "It's a shame, really. Maybe you should have your daddy fly a helicopter in to pick you up."

"That's enough, man," said Skye.

"I know you, Skye," said Wyatt. "Don't think I don't."

"Do you?" said Skye.

"You're friends with Royal and Chase, right?"

"So?"

"Yeah. I know you," said Wyatt.

"Great. Glad we got that out of the way."

"I don't know why you think you're in charge of our group. Is it because you roll with the soccer team? That doesn't make you worth anything on this river. So don't tell me what to do—*man*—but please, keep using the overly masculine language of the bros."

"Hey, tell me something," said Skye. "Why do you even bother with school? Don't you have enough generators and canned food to last a lifetime? Why do you even come to town? You should just stay in the sticks and make friends with your horses. I mean, would anybody even notice if you just disappeared one day?"

"C'mon, Skye," I said.

"And stop harping on Shelby. You don't know her," said Skye.

"Yeah. I do," said Wyatt. "I know all of you."

"No, you don't," said Shelby.

The driver cleared his throat, cutting the tension in the van. "So, uh, plan on no service for five days."

"Look," I said, hoping to change the direction of the conversation. "Wixom's human-interest story assignment is a joke. People don't win Pulitzers for that crap. They win for features about important people, about groundbreaking issues. You don't see the staff at the *Washington Post* writing about their co-workers, or Rachel Kaadzi Ghansah writing about the proprietor of the local bakery, or Kathryn Schulz writing about our driver. No offense—" I waited on his name.

"Thatcher."

"Thatcher," I repeated. I was suddenly worried I'd revealed too much nerdiness in the first few minutes in a weak attempt at impressing them.

"What? Didn't anybody else read the assigned packet?" I asked.

Wyatt laughed again.

I looked out my window, trying to ignore the others, who were avoiding eye contact with me for obvious reasons.

"And yet, they award Pulitzers to cartoonists, right?" said Skye.

"So you read it?"

"I didn't say that," said Skye.

"Yeah. Okay. Editorial cartoonists. Look at Halpern and Sloan, detailing the struggles of a refugee family. It's not *Dilbert*—though that's a good strip, don't get me wrong."

"Still just trying to *get you* in general," said Skye.

"That makes two of us," I said. "But at least we can all agree about journalism, right? We all chose Wixom's class. Let's just keep it focused on that."

"I only took the class to boost my GPA," said Shelby. "Can't be that hard. My friend Lissy took Wixom's class last year and said it was easy as long as you make her think you're into it."

"Sounds like your relationship to half the soccer team, Shelby."

29

"Eat my face, Wyatt."

"Okay," he said. "But only at school so all your friends can watch and judge you for slumming."

"My parents made me take it so I had a full load," said Skye.

"Awesome. Glad we're all taking it for the right reasons," I said. "What about you, Wyatt?"

"Doesn't matter. Just trying to fill my schedule and get out of Idaho."

"Trying to boost that GPA to a 2.0, Wyatt?" said Skye.

"Exactly!" said Wyatt, mocking a cheery disposition.

"It does make things awkward," said Shelby. "Interviewing someone else in our group. Can't I just do a video piece about myself and how the trip changed me?"

"Shelby's onto something," said Wyatt.

"You're really going to be like this for five days?" she said.

"Hopefully we won't have to talk much once we get started," said Wyatt. He removed a comic book from his backpack and started reading.

We rode in silence for a stretch, then Thatcher killed the engine, and we all climbed out of the van to see a massive grouping of quaking aspens next to our drop-off point. Light shot over the rim of the canyon and down into a crack. We looked to be hundreds of feet above the water.

I thought, perhaps, that we'd just pulled over before taking a winding trail down to the water's edge, but a man was waiting for us at the edge with a harness on and webbing set up around a large, lodgepole pine. He had a neatly trimmed beard and wore a Hells Whitewater Tours hat with stitched water rushing over the logo.

"Welcome," he said. "I'm Sawyer."

"We're the rafting group," said Shelby, "not the climbing group."

"I know," he said.

"Wow. I hate my parents," said Shelby.

"Do they often present you with two options and give you the one you don't want?" I said, unsure of why she was so upset.

"I didn't want to be here at all. I didn't want to get wet, and I didn't want to climb, either. But Wixom met with my parents, and this was the decision." She shot Wyatt a look before saying, "Horseback riding would have been just fine, thanks."

I felt like saying, "You're welcome," but I didn't want to get off to a rocky start. Well, I didn't want to make things worse, which was a distinct possibility. Rappelling was enough of a rocky start.

Thatcher spoke up. "We have to rappel down to the drop-in site. Your guide is waiting for you. We'll lower your gear first, and then send you on your way. We thought this would be easiest for everybody, rather than hiking down." He walked around to the back of the van to gather our belongings.

"He's talking about me," said Skye. "I'm *everybody*."

"That fits," said Wyatt. "Just glad you recognize you think that way."

"Skye with an *e*," I said, shaking my head. "Making everybody rappel so you don't have to hike."

"But I didn't sign up for rappelling," Shelby whined again.

Wyatt responded, "None of us signed up for anything. But this looks pretty cool. It's not like we're crazy-far up anyway.

Should be fun. Get over it." And then he trained his voice to a whisper. "Look at the light hitting that rock."

"What?" said Shelby.

"Nothing. Just roll with things instead of getting upset about everything. I'm sure they'll have a rest stop along the river where you can get a mani-pedi."

"I'll *roll with things* as long as you promise to stop pestering me," she said.

"Whatever," said Wyatt, his attention returning to the light on the rocks.

We waited for thirty minutes as each bag was tied to the climbing rope and let down slowly. Thatcher and Sawyer were adamant about us using the dry-bags they supplied to pack only what we needed for the first two full days, and Skye was adamant about that including his fly-fishing rod.

I didn't care about wearing the same swimsuit or sweater for the entire week, though I packed a couple so I had options. I liked having options. They said we needed to pack extremely light, and that they would bring our bags with the rest of our gear and meet us on the second *full* day, or day three overall.

The guide was gathering the things below and loading the raft so we'd be ready to set off immediately. Well, immediately after an eight-hour car ride and a thirty-minute van ride and a rappel—that kind of immediately.

Wyatt walked off the edge quickly, hopping out from the wall in a seated position, the rope whirring through the belay device as the canyon sucked him down into its greedy arms.

Skye went next and took his time. While he was adjusting

the harness, his shorts pulled up so his upper thighs were showing. I saw a faint tan line.

"Don't get any ideas, Indie," he said, noticing my stare. "I'm
not *that* easy. Well, okay, maybe if you keep smiling at me like
that."

I hadn't even realized I was smiling. There was something
about the way he talked, the way his words curled around one
another like river water around giant boulders.

"Are you always this audacious?"

"Did you just synonym me and think it would work?"

For a moment, I stared at Skye and didn't know what to say.
How many times had I been in a situation in which I didn't have
an immediate reply and was not two steps ahead of the person
I was talking to? Never. I had to change that "never" to "once"
after what Skye said, and looking at him made me wonder if
that "once" might change to "all the time." I was thrilled by the
idea of being stumped. It was like the Sunday crossword, only in
person. So many questions in front of me, so many options for
answers, down and across.

I was ashamed of myself for judging Skye, thinking he
wouldn't be able to keep up with me, thinking his mind was
one-track and built for soccer only. Skye. So many questions
leading to answers I didn't have. I was puzzling together a response, and he knew it, and yet I wanted that moment to last
for the rest of the day.

"Plucky, cocky, cheeky, brash?" I rattled them off.

"Criminal overuse of synonyms."

"How did I synonym you? I didn't know that was a thing,"
I said.

"You already asked me about being forward."

"Different word."

"Same idea," he said.

"Yes, but you didn't really give me an answer, did you?"

"I didn't have to. It's who I am. I've always been four words."

"Forwards?" I said.

"No, *four words*: forward, friendly, formidable, and frank."

"Thanks, Frank," I said. "This is going to be a long five days."

He was quick about his rappel, and his smiling face disappeared over the ledge and into a grouping of pines and a stripe of shade. He knew exactly what he was doing, prosthetic leg or not.

Shelby took what felt like, well, my entire life. She kept adjusting her clothing in the harness, asking Thatcher exactly how to stand and wondering about the exact length of the rope and how many things could possibly go wrong.

"What?" she snapped at me. "Why are you looking at me like that? You think you'll do better?"

I put my hands up and stepped back, even though I was already pretty far from her position.

"Just watching. Didn't mean anything by it."

"Sorry. Wyatt is just irritating, is all. And now I'm all edgy."

"I get it. But let's be friends first, and then move on to the whole enemy thing. I don't know you, but I'd rather start there instead of the reverse."

"Deal," she said, before turning to talk to Sawyer again. "Will my hair get stuck in this contraption? This is hell," she said, not waiting for a response from Sawyer or Thatcher. "I'm literally in hell."

"Well, technically you're on the lip of it. You have to rappel to be in it. Or, in its canyon, I guess I should say," said Sawyer.

She adjusted her hair seventeen times, checking every pin and clip and band. So irritating. And incredibly annoying. All the synonyms for being the worst. When she finally gathered the strength to step off the ledge, she asked if I'd film her on her phone as she walked down the wall.

I felt like I'd turned forty-five by the time I harnessed up, but I couldn't bring myself to immediately step off the ledge either. I regretted judging Shelby for taking her time. Maybe she was dealing with things like I was? Sawyer and Thatcher watched as I adjusted my harness as an excuse, as a way to stall, while I considered exactly what I was doing by dropping into that canyon.

They say rivers churn with an immeasurable power. They say Mom's body was irrecoverable because of that force. They say after a year stuck deep in those waters that her body was now part of the river, part of the silt billowing beneath each darting fish. They say a lot, I guess. But it was time for me to say something. And I'd start by saying it with my body. With that in mind, I stepped off the edge and into my grief. I felt the canyon salivate, open its mouth, and swallow me whole.

I was shocked by the sharp decline in temperature as I rappelled through what seemed like an invisible ceiling trapping the cool air near the river. I imagined grief lurching after me, grabbing at my ankles, licking its lips and watching me cringe as I focused on the rope in front of my face and how it would disappear over the ledge and leave me alone in the void.

The rock was gritty, and I stopped at one point to rest my fingers on a crimp, testing the feel. When my feet hit soft soil, I leaned against the cool rock wall of the canyon and undid the harness. The afternoon light was washing through the river as I stepped out of the shadow cast by the wall. Everyone else had loaded up and was waiting as I shuffled to the water's edge.

The overhanging walls, the towering pines, the snaking river—it was like I was on some other planet. The panoramic wonder felt enormous, beyond scale, without equal.

The guide was setting my duffel into place and latching it down, and I saw his gray ponytail and the way his massive, white beard haphazardly shot in every direction. Perhaps the beard is what caused me to do a double take, then a triple take, wondering exactly what I was seeing. And if what I *was* seeing was, in fact, real. But my hesitation only allowed this man, this monster, to speak first.

"I can't believe it," he said. "Indiana Lutz. The gods have been good to us."

I had no words for the man standing in front of me.

"This will be a time of healing. Let's get on the water."

I felt something rise in my throat. I didn't respond. I walked back to the canyon wall, but the rope was now absent, the harness was now gone, and the van and Thatcher and Sawyer up top had certainly disappeared around some bend, headed off into Nowheresville. I leaned my forehead against the stone.

Nash.

The name pinged around in my head, growing less

recognizable with each repetition of it from my open mouth, my gaping mouth, my cavernous maw. Just the sound of his name evoked some clawing animal, some rip in the fabric of life.

Reality snagged like a fishing line in the brush on the bank. Everything felt surreal. Heat rose to my face, and a distinct pain in my chest—a pinched pain—pulsed and spread like a stroke of lightning into each limb, the nerves pricking the skin as the circuit stretched beneath my withering shell.

My hands shook; my legs quivered as if I stood on quicksand. I felt something stirring inside of me: two years of questions.

"I can't do this," I said.

I repeated those words. I swallowed half those words so they didn't come out as a shout, as a bark. It was as if my anger had taken on life, coursing through my body, and was attempting to stomp me into the earth. My shaking knees finally buckled, and I sat on the ground and wiped away the hot tears on my face. I couldn't let anybody see what I was feeling.

The sand was cool beneath my legs, and the pines swayed in a small breeze coming off the water. I looked at the green needles stabbing the distant sky.

I can't do this.

I stared at the rocks at my feet for two minutes, and then it all came to me like the rapid recoil of a gun. The hammer came down, the powder ignited, and I knew that what I was seeing and hearing and feeling was real. My vocal folds began to vibrate, stretched thinly over my larynx, and the moment the vibration reached the back of my teeth and the opening of my mouth, the force and rupture of sound was sucked up into a cough, a hack, instead of a scream.

Nash Wilmer walked around the corner where the shrubbery hid me from the raft and the others waiting. He stood over me with his hands on his hips. His eyes were sharp and his body lean and his skin sunbaked, wrinkled beyond what I remembered. He must have been fifty, same age as Mom—well, what she would have been. What she *should* be. Chums wrapped around his neck held his sunglasses against his threadbare tank top.

"Everything okay?"

"It hasn't been okay for about two years now."

He sighed heavily and turned back. "We'll be ready when you are. I've been waiting for this moment, just like you," he said. He glanced back at me. "I didn't run away from Driggs, like they say, you know. I came here to start my own outfit. It had nothing to do with her."

"*Her* name is *Joyce*," I said. "*Was* Joyce."

"No, still is," he said. "And I think she'd want us to be here together. I'm off to the raft. We'll wait for as long as you need. It really is nice to see you, Indiana."

"Indie."

"Right. Okay, Indie."

I watched him walk back to a raft where three people I hardly knew—and didn't care to know—were waiting for me to make a decision, to tuck this reluctance away and move forward. Had Nash not been there, perhaps I would have continued to think the canyon was the most beautiful place I'd ever seen.

Leaves quivered in the breeze. I stared at my feet and curled my hands into the soft ground, digging, hoping I could open up the world and fall into the hot, roiling, melting center like a coin tumbling into a well, left there for good.

It was only day one of five, and I had no service in the canyon. No way out but through. Because rivers run through things. So does grief. Everyone will give you a different number for how many stages of grief there are, but there is only one way to conquer it, and that's to run through it, not around it.

And I had no choice but to ride the river with Nash—the man who just as well could have been wearing an executioner's hood. The man responsible for my mother's death.

THREE

Sirens—daughters of the river god. They were said to lure sailors to their deaths. In Greek mythology, the sirens' enchanting voices and mesmerizing songs were, like, outrageously attractive. Odysseus was smart enough to tie himself to the mast so he could resist their song. His men put beeswax in their ears so they wouldn't hear them. How was I to know I should have told my parents to cover their ears when I was born? How was I to know that my song would be their end—that the blue would take them, just in different ways? I may not be beautiful like a siren, but like them, everything I love must leave me or die.

I felt calmer in the boat as I watched the blue water curl in on itself and listened to the waves topple over after dipping and swaying around the boulders.

Our first campground was less than an hour away on the water, and nobody said much, other than Nash detailing the parts of the raft and how to handle the oars and mentioning something about it being bear country and to keep our eyes peeled for signs of them. He said he'd give us the full safety talk the next morning when things really got kicking, but for now we were just floating to a campsite nearby with lots of sand and shade. I took note of the gear tied down, the oars in their locks, the guide rope clinging to the outside of the rig.

I'd already asked Nash if he could radio out, and he tried, but his radio wasn't working. My phone wasn't working. Shelby's phone wasn't working. Nash said something about poor reception, the radios being shoddy, and the satellite phone being locked away only for emergencies. Wasn't this an emergency? Couldn't I make a case for this as, ultimately, the very definition of an *emergency*?

Asking about the radio had been my last recourse anyway, my last try, and I wasn't about to talk to him again. At least not that first day. I didn't feel I could justify the satellite phone request, so I decided to stick it out, trying not to think of Grandpa and Bury humming their way home.

I focused on trying to breathe deeply and imagining the knots in my intestines untangling. I was officially stuck on the river trip from hell. Excuse me, *through* hell—and the canyon where it kept its bluest river. Wyatt commented on the soft afternoon light to Nash, which surprised me, but I guess he didn't care to talk to anybody else. Shelby was filming it all, as usual. It was odd that I already had an "as usual" for someone, but Shelby was never off her stupid phone.

"It's going to get dark fast, as you can already see," said Nash, "so I'll make sure to set up your tents first. Then, I'll have you get the briquettes going and assign everybody else their jobs and we can get the food all set. Drink water. Lots of it. Your pee should be clear and copious."

"Gross," said Shelby.

"He's right," said Wyatt. "We need to be prepared for anything. Stay hydrated and walk around the camp so you know your surroundings. It's stupid to just set up a tent and sleep without knowing where the exits are or what weapons are available."

"Right. All these exits," said Skye, sidling off the raft and pointing up at the canyon walls.

"Can you guys let me get a video going before Nash sets up the tents? I don't want them in my shot. Wait," said Shelby, pulling her hair over her left shoulder, a tic or ritual or habit I was beginning to pick up on. "Maybe it's best with the tents in the shot. More authentic."

"What exactly are you trying to do?" I asked.

"Creating a social media following isn't easy," she said. "Like I said earlier."

Nash finished pulling the raft in. We were all on shore. He unlatched the gear and dropped it into the sand, which had been dimpled by the wind and droplets of water. We'd had an extremely dry summer, but the river was dam-controlled, so the rapids were still expected to be up to class IV. Hint: massive as hell. The foreboding clouds lurching overhead made the small campsite look ominous, but there was no rain.

Wyatt dropped his bag onto the sandy bank and eyed his surroundings.

Skye smiled cursorily at me as Nash helped him with his bag.

"I'll set up my own tent," I said. "Thanks."

Nash waved me on, probably already tired of my rightful anger.

Wyatt and I walked a hundred yards from the raft, looking for good tent sites. I figured if I was going to be stuck out-doors, I should stick close to the guy who knew how to prep for doomsday or the zombie apocalypse or whatever was going to bring the whole world to ash and chaos. Probably robots with super-advanced AI, if I had to guess. But I also knew the most about Wyatt, which was still almost nothing. And I was curious.

He sloughed his bag off his shoulder, and I saw a flash of metal where the zipper parted.

"Did you bring a freaking gun?" I said, trying to stay calm.

He laughed. "No. It's a hatchet. Stupid not to bring them, really. But I considered bringing a gun."

"Them? Like more than one?"

"That's usually what 'them' means. They're throwing hatch-ets. It's not a big deal. Hey, this way, I'll fit into what Skye and Shelby think of me by bringing primitive weapons."

I watched as my response options ticked right below Wyatt's face. I shook my head, as if that would somehow help, like I could shake the sand around in an Etch A Sketch. I'd been trying that for years, but it never helped, and yet I persisted. Definition of insanity, right?

"Well, just keep them in the bag, man."

"Of course. But you have to do something for me."

"Shoot."

"Don't talk like Skye and his thuggish goons, please. Drop the 'man' business."

"Deal."

"If I don't need to use these, I won't. But I'll probably practice with them one night when we have some downtime," he said, hefting a hatchet in his hand.

"Your dad teach you how to throw them?"

Wyatt looked at me, his face saying *Are you kidding me?* I guess it was a dumb question, knowing what little I did about his dad.

"He's only taught me about the kind of people who need to have hatchets thrown at them. But I'll stick to logs. These are only for protection and fun anyway."

Wyatt undid his bun, mussed it, and then tied it back in a ponytail and paused. His sighs echoed in the shade of the ponderosa pines. Spotted shadows gathered on the canyon floor.

"Sorry, that's a little much. But he's not easy on me. I'm sure you've heard him. You and your grandpa are close enough you can probably hear the bad nights. Even the good nights are probably too noisy with his drinking and shouting about football. He loves Boise State football more than he loves me, but I've come to terms with it."

I didn't know how to respond, so I stepped aside into a nice opening and Wyatt came right behind. We ducked below a branch, and Wyatt moved a few rocks and brushed the site with his foot.

"This is good. Not many prickly pear cacti nearby. We can both fit here." His face got red, and he shuffled back to his bag. "I mean, if you want to be near me. I don't snore or anything. I don't mind being alone. It's not a big deal. In fact, it's probably best I'm alone."

"No. I want to be here. This is great," I said.

Seeing Wyatt's smile made me feel good. There was something so soft about him, so sweet, and yet the exterior suggested everything but that.

He helped me set up my tent in no time. It was a snug place to sleep, but it's not like the raft had tons of room for giant tents. Nash had already explained that he ran a lean outfit, so we would not be glamping by any means. I was surprised he knew that word, but it made sense. He only had a few guys and gals and a few rafts, and oars are freaking expensive. Just one oar cost over five hundred bucks. That was according to Wyatt—how he knew, I didn't ask.

Knowing that our guide was running a small outfit on a tight budget meant nobody was all that excited about the food. Until we saw it. We gathered around the fire, where Nash was taking bags out of the "dry" cooler and the chilly bin—the one that held all the perishable stuff.

He took out three Dutch ovens and assigned us our individual duties for the night. I was in charge of getting briquettes going and setting them under the ovens, which was super easy. Skye and Shelby were on prepping food and washing dishes downstream. Wyatt was on groover duty.

That's something every rafter gets to know about right away—the groover. It was really just an ammo can that was placed in a spot far from camp where we could do our business and return with lines etched into our thighs where we rested our butts on the dang thing. It was small and awkward, and I wasn't looking forward to my turn on "groover duty."

"So, where do you want me to set up our toilet?" Wyatt said to Nash.

"Make sure it's somewhere scenic," said Skye.

"Planning on it," said Wyatt. "I'll have it overlooking the water with a nice view of the distant peaks, just for Shelby."

"Just make sure it's private," I said.

Wyatt walked away into the trees and around where the river bent toward the dying light. Nash pulled out some Hawaiian sweet rolls and some veggies. Shelby stared into her phone's small screen, recording Skye prepping a peach cobbler and some barbecued chicken. She coughed as the smoke switched directions with the slight breeze that was whispering through the pine needles.

"This is the worst," she said through a wheeze and a half-cough. Her eyes were watering, and she stepped into the pines and continued hacking. "Guys, this is why I don't camp."

I turned because I thought she was talking to us, but nope, she was talking to her phone. Those "guys" were her followers, her crew, her squad, her fam.

Nash looked up as I stepped closer to the fire to carry more briquettes to the ovens. Wyatt was adjusting the coals on the lid of the ovens, turning them, ash dusting off in flakes.

"All set up?" Nash asked me. "Rain-fly on?"

"I'm not a child."

"Just checking," Nash said. "I wouldn't expect rain, but best to be safe. Forecast looks good for this week."

"Right."

"Dinner should be ready in thirty," said Skye.

I hunched my shoulders against the wind and pulled up my

hood. I was in board shorts with a swimsuit underneath, and I had a massive hoodie to keep me warm at night. Wyatt returned through the pines and sat across the fire from me. Skye sat down and then patted the boulder next to him, but I shook my head. I was just fine where I was, thanks.

"Okay, team," said Nash. "We'll talk river rules in the morning. For now, relax by the fire and get ready for the ride of your lives."

"Or our demise," I said.

Nash sighed and slouched and walked to the ovens to help Shelby with the charcoal and plating the food.

"Why are you so tough on the guy, Indie? How do you two know each other, anyway?" Skye's hesitation grew into a gaping curiosity. "*Do* you know him?"

"Sure," I said.

"He didn't tell us anything while we waited for you at the drop-in. He said you needed a moment to fix your swimsuit. But, as the son of a divorce, I know how to read subtext. I think. Correct me?"

I had a few options appear before me:

1. *Tell Skye the whole story, with Nash in earshot to edit my recounting of every detail, and set us off on a path of shame and guilt and regret, especially with the one feeling guilt being the only one capable of safely getting us out of the canyon.*
2. *Tell him I hate beards and river guides over fifty.*
3. *Deviation, about-face.*
4. *Ask Wyatt if I could borrow a hatchet for a minute.*

5. *Tell Skye my swimsuit was lodged in places where it was difficult to un-lodge and wait for his face to change color.*
6. *Ask Shelby if she could teach me how to use a selfie stick.*

Not great options, and I chose to go with my favorite anyway: number 3.

"It's true what they say about teenagers. That's all."

"That they hate river guides? Or that they hide their luscious locks in ponytails to avoid a constant barrage of admirers?"

"Is this how you win over all the girls?" said Wyatt. "Cheap comments and that patented smile of yours? If it wasn't so fake, I might believe you."

"I wasn't talking about your ponytail, Wyatt," said Skye.

"I can't believe I'm on a river with this guy," said Wyatt.

I waited because Wyatt looked like he had more to say. Skye's grin became a grimace in short order, but he didn't respond. He then rested against the boulder that curved up against his back.

"I wasn't talking to you anyway, cowboy," said Skye.

"Don't."

"Don't what?" said Skye.

"Don't say that," Wyatt said, shaking his head.

His quads tensed, and I realized he was half-standing, waiting for Skye to say something else. I don't know why "cowboy" did the trick when the ponytail comment hadn't, but maybe a fight would get them to cool off a little. I thought of standing back and letting the emotions rise, but Nash came back over.

"Everything okay here?"

"We're good," said Skye. "Right, Wyatt?"

"Right," Wyatt said. "We're good, *man*." He stood and walked to the river with what looked like a sketchbook in his hand.

Skye moved around the fire to sit next to me. His gait was hitched a bit, because of the prosthetic, and I noticed he kept touching it, almost like a mindless tic, checking if it was still there or something.

"I know, according to gender roles, I'm supposed to be more stoic and all. But I can't. It's just not me."

"Right," I said. I tried to hide my flushed face, and coughed as the smoke drifted past me. I exaggerated the cough and waved my hand in front of my face to sell it. "What happened to your leg? Can I ask?"

"Nice deflection."

"Thanks."

Nash was at the Dutch ovens, plating dinner. Shelby was helping with the coals as Wyatt stepped from the river and closed his book. He trudged over just as Skye started to describe how he lost his leg. Nash and Shelby joined us and set plates on a makeshift table—a sunbaked log split in half and spread over two rocks.

Skye said that the whole thing started eight months earlier in southern Utah. He and his buddy Lewis had taken their climbing gear to Moab to ascend a series of elite routes: Like a Prayer, From Switzerland with Love, Prosthetics (ironically), and Death of a Cowboy, among other intense climbs. They packed up after their last climb of the week—a two-pitched climb called Hot Pork Sundae—finishing just as the stars began showing off above them in all their patterned light. Skye and Lewis cruised home through the crumbling rock of the Utah desert that looked more like Mars than Earth.

Lewis began flagging but didn't say anything to Skye, who was already asleep, preparing to drive the last leg of the trip. Well, that's how Skye told it—he really didn't know because he was asleep. He only woke when the car flipped. It came to a stop right-side up in a drainage ditch off the highway in Price Canyon, smoke rising from the twisted metal.

The car sat next to the railroad tracks, and the ambulance was there before Skye realized that, while he was able to freely move his legs, one was significantly lighter. He passed out shortly after the ambulance arrived, and almost bled out on that roadside, but a helicopter from the nearby Provo hospital flew over the mountain, dipped into the canyon, and got Skye to a surgical team.

"When the car flipped, it split the metal into a perfect scythe, exactly where my left knee rested. It sheared off my leg below the knee like it was cutting through butter."

Skye turned his leg in the firelight and showed us the prosthetic.

"I was flown to the hospital, but they weren't prepared to deal with this kind of savagery. I suspect few hospitals would be. I'd lost so much blood that they had to focus on me before the leg. The doctors worked on me for two days straight, attempting to reattach the limb, and I watched as my toes went black during recovery. They said they only see that kind of amputation every couple years or so, and it sometimes takes, though the nerves never fully recover. But none of that worked for me. No bone, no nerves, no nothing. As you can see."

Shelby visibly cringed and then stuck her tongue out, giving a face to the things we were all feeling inside.

"I told them to take the thing before I had to see the rest of my leg die and blacken like a scorched log."

The fire popped right then, and sparks floated into the air almost on cue, as if dramatizing the image of the leg, the loss of soccer and rock climbing and, well, everything Skye once knew.

"That's pretty gnarly," said Wyatt, waving smoke away from his face.

"Yeah," said Skye. "Pretty much."

Skye gave Wyatt a quick nod, and I felt the tension drop between them. I imagined myself shouting: *We're back to DEFCON 5—normal peacetime status. Keep up the good work, team!*

I inched closer and let my shoulder rest against Skye's. It was a bold move, but it felt right, and he didn't budge.

Shelby was staring at Skye's leg, still in shock from the story, her perfect hair falling over her perfect shoulders, the rest of her body continuing that statuesque, refined look right down to her perfect feet. It made me wonder why Skye was flirting with me and not her.

"You know, weirdly, when I think back on it, it reminds me of one of your mom's physics lectures," Skye said to me.

"That is weird," said Wyatt. "I'd be thinking of robot legs, and then the robot army that will ultimately be our demise."

"I thought it would be zombies," I said.

"No. That's just for fun. The robot army thing is real," said Wyatt. "Just ask Elon Musk."

"Who?"

"The SpaceX guy. He's going to get us to Mars and make it livable and help us escape from Earth before the apocalypse— which will totally happen. Trust me."

"Why did it make you think of school?" asked Shelby.

"Not school," said Skye. "Just that one class. I've had plenty of time to think about stuff, being homeschooled and all."

"You knew my mom?" I said.

"Everyone at school knows your mom," said Shelby. "She's, like, the best teacher at Teton High. Everybody knows that."

"Was."

"What?" said Shelby.

"She *was* the best teacher. Not *is*."

I had a slight feeling I'd end up liking Shelby, even if she did always tell me that I should know things I didn't know. I knew there was a lot I had been missing because I'd been stuck in the strainer of my own life, caught between a rock and, well, another rock.

"Why did you think about my mom's class?" I asked Skye.

I eagerly anticipated this memory of my mother that I didn't yet have access to, as if each memory were a coin I could roll through my hands and flip over my knuckles and then cash it in for one moment of pure joy when everything would stop and she'd be alive again.

But hearing about her also felt like each memory, each coin, was being spent and I'd never get it back. As if by storing those memories in my bank, I could preserve her, keep her safe inside my head like she was the day I saw her last.

"'And yet, it moves,'" said Skye.

"I remember that class," said Wyatt.

"You two had a class together?" said Shelby.

"It's not a big school," said Skye.

"Yeah," said Wyatt, "and even guys like Skye need grades in order to graduate."

"Ha ha," said Skye.

"Granted, they're usually not good grades, right, Skye? But that's why the athletes are lucky their coaches pull double duty and teach so many of their classes. Otherwise, Skye might end up like me: poor trailer trash, canning my own food."

"I don't think of you that way," said Shelby.

"You sure?" asked Wyatt.

Shelby was silent.

"That's what I thought," said Wyatt, quietly.

"'And yet, it moves' was something Galileo said," said Skye, trying to change the conversation back to my mom's physics class. "Your mom said people argue over the truthfulness of the account, but she still tells it because of what it teaches."

"It's bunk," said Wyatt. "Sorry, but there's no way he said that. I looked up a bunch of theories, and I'm pretty sure it's false. Almost certain."

"Why does it matter if he said it or not?" said Shelby.

"Because if he said it, and it was heard, and it was recorded, then he was basically telling the people who wanted him jailed that he'd lied to the pope or whatever. He wouldn't risk putting himself out there like that. Doesn't make sense. He gives some big speech about how he's sorry he lied and that the earth really doesn't move around the sun and that the pope is right and the church is correct, and then he walks outside and says, 'And yet, it moves'? I don't buy it."

"You don't have to buy it," said Skye. "I just like the idea of it. Can I at least have that?"

Wyatt was silent, waiting for Skye to continue.

Nash got up from the log and checked on the Dutch ovens. I'd forgotten he was there.

"And what was the deal with Galileo?" Shelby said.

"So, hundreds of years ago the pope got upset with all the scientists who were looking into the big bang," said Skye. "He said that researching that was basically attempting to look into the work of God, so he put the kibosh on it. Well, rumor is that Galileo presented the idea of the heliocentric solar system, got totally chewed out for it, and then made that comment afterwards. I know Wyatt doesn't think he said it, but I like to think he did. I think he confessed to being wrong, even though he wasn't, to save his life. I think he said it to himself, later, even if nobody else heard it."

"Then there wouldn't be a record of it," said Wyatt.

"Doesn't matter, man. Mrs. Lutz likes the story, and I like it too—the idea of Galileo saying to himself, 'And yet, it moves.' Like, sure, I'll let you keep your worldview, but just know I've seen the thing move and I know life isn't what you think it is—or thought it was—and it won't ever be because I looked off into space and figured some big things out and the world will never be small again like it once was. It can't be. I love that."

"Liked," I said.

"What?"

"She *liked* to believe the idea. You said *likes*."

I was suddenly angry I hadn't been there, that I hadn't taken my mother's physics class. I'd taken another general education course because it felt weird being in a class with my mother, but I'd regretted it every day since she died.

I figured I had time to take the class later, but I didn't. That's how time works. It's a river that flows right past you. It doesn't wait for you. You're lucky if you manage to dip your hand in it and feel the cool currents as it passes.

Skye shrugged. "I thought it was a good lesson in how we can be wrong. Sure, everyone in heaven and earth can believe a theory, but in the end, it's what we see. And Galileo saw something that proved the earth moves around the sun."

"The worst part about that is how long it took the church to apologize," said Wyatt. "Even if the whole story isn't true, we know Galileo was, like, shafted big-time. He'd been right the whole time."

"How long did it take?" said Shelby.

"They apologized, like, twenty years ago. Only, what, four hundred years too late," Wyatt said.

"Sounds about right," I said.

"Dinner is ready," said Nash, waving us over. "Nice work on the Dutch ovens, guys. This is how God intended us to eat, I believe. Even in a canyon."

"Even in hell," said Shelby.

"C'mon, Shelby, it's not that bad," said Skye.

"Wait till you get to the cobbler," said Nash.

We all stood to plate our chicken and sides and cobbler. I sat by the fire with my food and thought about what Skye had said. Was I putting too much weight behind my version of how Mom died, or was Nash holding fast to an outdated idea of how the sun orbited around the world—how he was at fault for my loss and how my orbit was now much smaller and with fewer planets?

I was planet-less but for Grandpa and Bury. And how was I to confront that? Confront Nash? Anger twisted in my gut. What was I doing on this sandy beach in a canyon miles away from any sense of home or, in my condition, any sense of sense? It was senseless. I was incensed.

After dinner, I walked to my tent and grabbed the crossword puzzle book off the top of my duffel. I clicked on my head-lamp as night descended, the darkness moving into the canyon and settling like silt at the bottom of the river. I heard Shelby and Skye cleaning up the gear and moving their tents closer to the fire. It seemed we'd formed alliances without really trying: Shelby and Skye, Wyatt and Indie.

I couldn't see anything outside because of the rain-fly, so I figured I'd stick to the words and doze off. I didn't care to be by the fire roasting marshmallows, even if it was what Nash called "part of the evening river experience." I'd had enough of "the experience." In fact, I'd grilled Nash about my exit options at dinner. Apparently, we didn't have any options until day three, and even then it would be tricky.

I flipped to a Sunday puzzle and stared at the clue: "Good name for a dyslexic hibernator?" I cruised through options. *Bear*. Not a name. Plus, the answer was only three letters long. What else hibernated? Then I realized it wasn't the animal, but the place. Ned. Got it. After five more clues, my eyes got heavy.

Several hours later, I woke up to a noise. I was cold, and my bag wasn't zipped up. The puzzle book was on my pillow, my pen next to it, and my face probably had clues imprinted on it because I'd been sleeping on the pages. My headlamp was still on—not good for the batteries.

At first, the noise was just a soft rustle in the pines outside the tent. Wyatt must have been a heavy sleeper, because I didn't hear any movement in his tent, which was just five feet from mine. Then the noise grew louder. Everything slowed down, it seemed, and I felt the beat in my chest rise to my throat. It sounded more and more like a hog snorting, but the size of it was too large for that.

Whatever-it-was brushed up against my tent. I didn't know what to do. The snorting continued, and then turned into a growl, but deeper than what I was expecting, like a wet bark. My hands started shaking. Adrenaline was coming off me in waves.

Options:

1. *Try to think of large words and play an anagram game— rearrange letters to distract myself.*
2. *Shout for Wyatt to wake up, then ask if he heard any- thing.*
3. *Look up at the tent fly and worry for three (or four, or five) more hours until the sun comes up, while biting my nails and pulling my hair out and losing my mind.*

I didn't have time to make a decision because Wyatt shouted, "It's a bear! Stay in your tent!" Then I heard Wyatt's tent flap unzip as he shouted "Hey bear!" over and over, nearly screaming each word.

I turned my headlamp off and coiled my body into a small ball. I heard the bear lumber away after Wyatt shouted again. I wanted to unzip my tent and walk over to Wyatt, but I also didn't want to leave my tent, and I definitely didn't want to be left alone.

Decision made, I unzipped my tent and peeked out. With the starlight overhead, I could see surprisingly well.

I darted to Wyatt's tent, where he was sitting down, tying his shoes. He had a hatchet next to his feet. He stepped out of the tent and stood next to me.

"What the hell, Wyatt? Hatchets are small. Bears are large. It'd be like throwing a rock at a T-Rex."

"I just want to scare it before it gets to the food. Trust me, I don't plan on killing it with these things."

"Better than a stick, I guess. At least let me help," I said. "Give me the other one."

He hesitated. I couldn't see his eyes well, but I imagined he was surprised at my request. Even I was surprised at my request, at my willingness to confront something so formidable. Then I felt the cool metal of the handle in my palm.

"You know how to throw?"

"We're from Tetonia, *man*. It's like, you get teething toys, then you learn to fly-fish, then you learn to shoot, then you learn to throw sharp objects at people. I mean animals. I mean logs."

"Right. Fair enough. I should be able to come up on him from upstream and scare him with some shouting. Just don't throw the hatchet unless you have to—adrenaline can do strange things to people."

"Yeah," I said. "Like make them throw hatchets."

"I'm pretty good with this thing," he said, hefting the hatchet in his right hand.

"I don't doubt it."

I was bouncing on my toes without realizing it. Wyatt put his hand on my arm and whispered, "Relax. I still hear it."

I didn't, which was not good news, although didn't some part of me want to confront the thing? It was foolish to put myself in that kind of danger, but wasn't some small part of me hoping the bear would maul me so I could take a helicopter ride out of the canyon, away from the river and Nash and all thoughts of my dead mother? Maybe I just wanted to be hundreds of miles from the center of gravity, from the place my grief was born? Wasn't the bear-mauling kind of pain easier to deal with, anyway? I walked behind Wyatt in the odd half-light of the pine-covered campsite.

As we neared the sandy beach where the campfire was completely cooled, I saw a large black mass moving near our raft and considered darting back to my tent, but I didn't want to be alone.

"It's after the food," said Wyatt, pointing at the bags and boxes strewn across the ground. "I knew it." He looked at me as I bounced on my toes. "Don't worry, they're omnivores and don't usually threaten humans. My bet is he'll take to the river and swim across when I approach. I'm going to be super loud to make him run. Don't be scared."

"Hard not to be a little scared, Wyatt."

"Fair enough."

That was Wyatt's catchall phrase—as if life was giving him just enough not to complain, but not enough to make things easy. Maybe I was more in that boat than I liked to let on. I hated platitudes, but with Wyatt it felt different, like he was using it as a way of explaining himself.

Maybe by saying things were fair enough, he meant that no amount of complaining would change his situation, so why not call it "enough"? He had plenty of reasons, but he was bigger than those reasons, it seemed, from what I knew of him. And that still wasn't much.

I'd always struggled with recognizing the core in anybody else, like, what really drove them, what really motivated them. It was like I couldn't see the combustion engine inside the heart, so I assumed that all it took to get a hold on somebody was to look at them and listen briefly. Not a good philosophy. Still, it felt nice to recognize something in Wyatt even while scared out of my mind about the bear.

"You stay here," Wyatt said. "I'm going to sneak around that side and try to get it to run downstream."

"Perfect," I said. "We'll just meet up with it tomorrow night, then. Can you make sure to tell it where Nash is sleeping? Why can't I go with you? I don't want to be alone."

"The bear will wander somewhere else. He won't come back this way. He will get distracted or bored. Don't stress."

"*He* will? How do you know it's a 'he'? Is it because of the way the bear bottles up its emotions and acts tough even though it just wants to forage and write poetry?"

Wyatt didn't laugh, and I wasn't sure why. Instead, he took off without me into the trees, and I was left wondering if I'd made a huge mistake not just in what I'd said but in getting out of my tent in the first place.

I considered returning to my tent, but what if the bear

backtracked and found me alone? I squatted on my heels and listened, then scrambled closer to the tents of Shelby and Skye, thinking that even a warm body would be enough to drown out some of the fear roiling inside me.

I looked on as a giant mass in the distance nudged our raft and tore apart our food.

I began shaking their tents, whispering their names as loudly as possible, and telling them a bear was in our camp. I could hear Shelby and Skye moving around in their respective tents. Wyatt didn't show. I didn't hear him either.

The bear wandered from the raft to Nash's tent, which was right next to the water and about twenty yards upstream. I wanted to shout for Wyatt, but I didn't want to call any attention to myself. I also didn't want the bear to rip open Nash's tent and maul him. Well, maybe I did. Maybe a little.

But I knew that was wrong because whenever I thought of Mom, my moral compass knew exactly where to point. She was my lodestar. Justice would be done when Nash admitted to his wrongdoing, not with a life for a life. I knew that much, at least. But why not a small cut? Why not an injury just to remind him what he'd taken from me?

The bear was snorting and pawing at the ground near Nash's tent, so I stepped out of the cover and into the open space near the firepit. I was scared and felt goose bumps all over my body, but I didn't want anything to happen to Nash. And why not?

I still didn't see or hear Wyatt. Where was he? I stepped within twenty yards of the bear just as Skye unzipped his tent door behind me. I lifted the hatchet shoulder-high. If Wyatt wasn't going to scare it, I would have to. Just then, Wyatt started shouting, and I saw Nash's tent door unzip.

The bear stood on its hind legs and growled, then immediately landed on all fours and snorted. It quickly made an about-face and lumbered downstream just like Wyatt had said it would—*he* would.

Wyatt continued to shout and wave his arms in the air as he ran toward Nash's tent, and Nash turned on his headlamp and pointed it right at where I stood, the hatchet raised, my hands shaking.

I tended to present the illusion that I didn't know my way around a hatchet or a gun or a fly rod or the outdoors in general. But I was a deadeye with a rifle—with anything, really. I could catch a twenty-two-inch brown on a dry fly in one arcing cast, and I could hit a nickel at three hundred yards with my Winchester. I knew I could throw the hatchet twenty yards and bury it into anything standing or sitting. I wondered why I felt like I had to hide that stuff from people. Like, did somehow focusing on journalism mean I had to give up the other part of who I was?

The headlamp beam obscured most of Nash's body, but I knew he was staring right at me. Wyatt was five yards from Nash, breathing heavily after chasing the bear away. Nash kept whispering to me, as I stood with the hatchet raised, that the bear was gone, that we were safe, that we could—and should—get back to our tents, and that I only had to put down the hatchet.

Was all the fear finally catching up to me, unloading the adrenaline into my system in that moment, dropping the heavy cargo and leaving me motionless, speechless, in shock? Or did I really want Nash to feel that fear himself, for other reasons?

I thought of these things, but I also recognized I was only a few feet from the man who took my mother out of this world, and I had the power to seriously injure him with just one rotation of my arm and one flick of my wrist. Skye and Shelby walked up next to Wyatt, but didn't say anything.

"It's just me, Indie," said Nash. "We're all safe now. The bear is gone. It's over. You can put the hatchet down."

He held his hands out to his sides. I knew he was thinking exactly what I was in that moment because then he said, "She'd be so proud of you, Indie. You're brave. Just like her."

I dropped my arm and felt the weight of the hatchet pull at my wrist. I knew exactly how far it would have flown based on its weight. Just like I knew Nash hadn't been trying to send my mom into the next life without me. I knew he hadn't meant to do that. Scratch that—I *wanted* to know that he hadn't meant it. But right then, all I knew was that it had happened and I was there and she wasn't and the man responsible for all of it was a hatchet-throw away from me.

"Just like her," I said.

What I didn't say is that, just like her, I knew a coin flip had an expected probability of fifty percent. Why, then, did I feel my life had been all tails? Every outcome was equally likely, and yet my parents were gone, and I was on the river now with Nash. I'd flipped tails seventy-six times in a row, it seemed. Would this trip be seventy-seven?

The first law of probability—that one chance event has no effect on the next chance event and its result. Why, then, did

I feel that by making the decision to continue with the river trip instead of running for any possible exit, I was changing the course of everything?

"That bear was freaking huge," said Shelby, her hair disheveled and mussed.

I noticed Skye was standing next to her, but I didn't care. I had way too much adrenaline.

"Couldn't run very fast, either," said Wyatt.

But, adrenaline or not, I couldn't help myself when it came to double meanings, and I didn't feel like letting Nash off the hook that easily.

Nash pointed the headlamp at his hand, and I set Wyatt's hatchet into his wrinkled palm.

"Next one might be moving a little quicker," I said.

FOUR

'm prone to wander. I'm prone to outlandish claims and making poor decisions because I'm compulsive. I'm prone to stay close to those I love and question others and never turn that gaze inward. I'm prone to seek after a certain individuality, yet I still look to belong. I want to belong. And I'm prone to loneliness. I need company, and it might be important to know why.

One winter, when I was seven years old, snow had piled up on the sagging roof of our first house, on the very land where our current trailer sits. The log bench out front had at least six inches coating the faded rings. The driveway was cleared of any snow, the shovels resting against the cold wood of the front porch, the kicked-over can of embers burning bright overhead—not to get too poetic or anything. I mean, it was only a memorable night because of what happened at 3:00 a.m. beneath the floorboards: the heating coils drove lines of sparks through the wood like some gigantic sciatic nerve—a malfunction of amazing proportions.

Flames gathered and sucked in the oxygen of our quiet house. Minutes later, Mom was running and yelling because she couldn't find me and assumed I was already out of the blaze. The local fire department got there in time to witness the last moments of our little home.

But before it all went to ash, and before the firefighters could stop her, Mom ran back into the walls of heat. I was in my closet, huddled in the corner, a ball of curiosity and fear, choking on the smoke. I don't remember much more of that night, but I know Mom returned from the burn unit a few weeks later with black lungs and scars all over her back and chest and legs. And I remember seeing the snow shovels in the heap of soaked ash, hissing in the aftermath, in the wetness.

All that to say I was a wonderful mess myself, and not without my own issues. And maybe I wasn't the only one. I thought of that moment, of being huddled in a ball, of Mom's black lungs and scars, as I stood in the campsite with adrenaline dripping off my body. The only other time in my life when I'd felt such a massive dump of energy.

Night. A five-letter word for "sunless," "nocturnal," "a period of affliction," "opposite of day." There is a difference between saying the word and reading it on a page. It's like reading the word "soldering" and then hearing someone say it. That's how it felt to be around Skye. Like people could tell me all day what he was like or what he was supposed to be like or how popular he was or what made him *him*, and yet, when I was next to him, he was something else entirely. Maybe everyone is like that.

You can't separate the idea or the sound or the taste from the thing itself. It's like hearing someone talk about love, *say* love, but never live it. It's impossible to know it unless it becomes a river and carves into the rock and cuts deep canyons in your heart.

I was acutely aware of standing next to Skye as I surveyed the damage to our campsite.

The bear had completely ransacked our food. Our dry bin was torn to pieces—devoured. The cooler was still there, but all the bread and muffins and candy bars were demolished or gone entirely. What remained was torn or smooshed or half-eaten. We spent thirty minutes cleaning up what we could find while Nash repeated his safety speech about how we shouldn't have food in our tents and how to shout if we heard a bear and how we should sleep closer to one another the next night.

The chilly bin, with all of our eggs and meat and fluids, was still locked. At least that much worked in our favor. I remembered Nash telling Skye and Shelby to close the coolers when they were done and make sure they locked properly, but I didn't think it was because of bears. At least the bear only got one of the two.

As Nash droned on, I found myself standing next to Skye, waiting for everyone else to leave, and enjoying the fact a little when I realized he was also waiting.

I heard the various tents zip up in the distance, and neither of us said anything for a moment. That pause became interminable, like a person could live and grow and achieve all their hopes and dreams and then die having led a good life during that pause. That kind of pause. We were just standing there.

"So, did you used to work as a bodyguard for high-profile targets?" Skye said. "Or maybe you just practice throwing sharp things at night? Or both?"

I didn't know how to respond, so I just listened to the river roll over itself, the waters dipping and curving in the starlight. Rivers never sleep. I wasn't ready to either. I wasn't even close to being tired. I was bouncing on my toes again without realizing it, because I had so much adrenaline flowing through me.

"Want to walk down this beach and see if we can get a good view of the sky? Too many trees near the campsite," he said.

"I won't mention that I already have a good view of the sky—with an *e*."

"But you just mentioned it," said Skye.

"Yeah, but I said I wouldn't mention it, so it negated the rest of the sentence."

"I don't think that's how it works. Like when people say 'Needless to say' and then continue to say something . . . needless. It's ludicrous."

"Are you saying I'm ludicrous?" I said.

"Nope. You can't rap. I'm just saying that a construction of words that is really hiding the truth behind it is obnoxious. Are you a construction of words?"

"What else are we made of? We're just big bags of words."

"Maybe right over there is a good spot to stargaze?" said Skye. "I mean, I'd like to rest this bag of words for a while. Speaking of bags of words, you sure know how to carry your vowels."

He nodded at my feet, and I realized I was bouncing on my toes again. I tried to settle down as we made our way to a nice stretch of near-white sand. I was impressed by his agility with the prosthetic; I'd thought it would slow him down, but it rarely did. I watched him touch it again. We both lay on our backs and stared upward at the stars.

"Why are you doing this?" I asked.

"For credit in Wixom's class, for starters," he said.

"No. I mean, why are you with me right now, and not Shelby?"

"I'm interested in getting to know you."

"But Shelby's prettier," I said.

"Wow. So, you must be on board with what Wyatt thinks of me."

"Why did you mock Wyatt and not me? I live in the same kind of trailer as Wyatt. And my grandpa runs the mortuary, and people make fun of me all the time for that. Why not you?"

"I want to get to know you, like I said. Like I keep saying. People won't give me a chance to be somebody different."

We both stared upward and let the light show wash over us. I watched Skye touch his leg again, and tried to change the subject.

"There's the Big Dipper," I said. "Acting all big."

"And dipping," said Skye.

The stars were pinpricks of light, the Big Dipper tilting as if full of stars on the verge of flowing out, as if saying, "Drink me!"

We were quiet for another minute.

"Maybe it's best if we don't get to know each other too well," I said, unable to stay away from the idea.

"Why not?"

"Because what happens in a few weeks when we're back in school?"

He shifted in the sand, and we rested in silence for a beat.

"I don't know. That's part of the whole future thing. I have zero idea what it will be like," he said.

"You sure you won't just fall back in with your buddies and forget I exist?"

"I always knew you existed," he said.

"Really? Then name one person I hang out with at school."

He rested a beat and touched his leg again. "Wyatt?"

"That's what I figured," I said.

"C'mon, Indie, I just want to get to know you. It doesn't have to mean anything."

"So, you don't want it to mean anything?"

"That's not what I meant," Skye said.

"Yes, it is. Words can mean anything, especially what they're intended to mean when you say them. But look, I'm not mad. It's probably safer if we don't get to know each other all that well. That way you don't have to fake something you're not. That way we can keep our secrets and move on and be just fine. Everybody leaves, anyway."

"Great strategy," he said.

"I know."

"So, you're going to go through life and not get to know anybody at all?" said Skye.

"Worked for me so far," I said.

"Has it?"

Skye grabbed my hand, and I pulled mine away immediately.

I knew Skye as the soccer phenom, as the athlete with Division 1 potential, as the guy who planned on jetting from

Idaho as soon as he got that first offer, as the guy all of Shelby's friends were after.

I figured he had to hear how hard my heart was beating in that moment. I felt the beat in my chest, my neck, my arms, and down to my toes and back again. I felt like I had a separate heart for each limb, for each part of my body.

"You really *are* forward," I said.

"It's just holding hands. It doesn't have to mean anything. Needless to say, you are smart and fiery, and I like that."

"Yes, it *does* have to mean something. And those things are needless?"

"Just messing with you."

Stars wheeled overhead. We watched for a few minutes as some stars threw themselves into the blackness, and some proceeded unmoved in their brilliant light.

I listened to the water and remembered where I was, and some of the magic of the moment slipped away into the sounds of the river. I've heard the horrible, haunting suck of the strainer for the last two years. The fallen logs and the sleeper boulder beneath the roaring waters—right where my mother was pulled under and drowned.

After we got word of what happened, Grandpa drove out to the spot and camped on the river. He wouldn't let me go with him that first time. Said I was too young to see it, that she would be unrecognizable even if they could get her out. But it didn't end up mattering. The water was so high and she was so deep that the search and rescue crews had to wait for the dam levels to drop in order to get her body out.

But that was just it: her body was too deep. Even with lower water levels, they couldn't get to her. I remember staring at that water months later, when I finally visited the site, knowing she was stuck beneath it, and yet the river moved on like it always had and always would without a care in the world.

I was lost in that moment next to Skye, my mind reeling backwards, completely assailed by memory because of the river, when he spoke again.

"Were you and your mom close?" he asked.

I couldn't talk about that. "Why not Shelby?" I said instead.

"You really can't get over that, huh? I like Shelby," he said, "but not like that."

"Why? Did you date her best friend or something and now you can't date her because of it?"

He was silent. He didn't move. He didn't speak.

"Holy buckets. I knew it!"

"It's more complicated than that."

"Way to be predictable," I said.

"Thanks. But that's not why. I don't think it matters if I dated her best friend. Besides, that friend is in college now, and I'm still here. And I'm talking to you, not her."

"You *were* talking to me," I said as I stood and brushed the sand off my board shorts and sweater. "That's part of the whole past thing. I have a good idea of what Skye *was* like, so I know exactly what his future *will* be like."

I started walking away, knowing he was perfectly capable of returning to his tent on his own. I was drenched in confusion and I was annoyed and the adrenaline was still circling my heart and I wasn't sure I'd ever be able to sleep.

I had my crosswords in my tent, and I could work on those

until I fell asleep. I could try to think of all of the four- or five- or six-letter words for "confusion and regret," because I felt them all in that moment but didn't know what to say. Was I angry at Skye, or at the fact that I wasn't allowing myself to open up to him when he was clearly trying? Could I separate the two?

"I think we were supposed to be on this river together, Indiana," he said to my back.

I didn't turn. "I don't believe in coincidences," I said over my shoulder.

If I had turned, Skye would have been an outlined shadow against the backdrop of the river and pine and sky. I didn't turn, and I didn't stop until I was in my tent with my head on the pillow, the headlamp off, my heart pounding, heat burning in my chest and neck and face. Wyatt was snoring in his tent— another lie. My eyes got heavy, and I forgot about Skye as I turned on my back and felt the weight of the ring on my chest and thought about a great sink opening up in the sheet of space and swallowing me whole.

FIVE

When I emerged from my tent the next morning, I saw Nash salvaging the food we had missed the night before and throwing it in the twisted cooler. We still had meat and eggs and bacon, so that felt like a win.

But how on earth was I going to survive four days on a boat with a guy I was both attracted to and upset with, another guy who had a bag with throwing hatchets in it, and a girl who was my exact opposite?

I needed a new vacation. Oh, and a new life. What once seemed doable now seemed like a burden, like my friendship with Skye, if I could even call it a friendship. I was still upset about the night before, but that only seemed to fuel my determination to confront Nash. It was going to happen. It had to. Soon. Maybe today. I knew that much. I just didn't know how.

Maybe I'd been too hard on Skye. I wasn't sure how to process it all. Was there such a life as one without coincidence? If that were true, what did it mean that I was there, then, with Nash and the rest of our group? Don't stories go in a straight line? And why would I think Skye was any different just because he'd been in that accident? He was still trying to be a player, just like always, just like everything I'd always heard about him.

I walked to the river and stared at the mountains sawing away at the sky. I listened to the chirps of the birds and the water moving and the trees rustling in the wind. It was like the canyon was having a conversation with itself. I didn't want to butt in, so I headed to the campsite, where our makeshift table was covered in muffins, one can of orange juice, and two oatmeal packets with some hot water and bowls and spoons. Apparently Nash had recovered enough for a shareable breakfast.

After grabbing some eggs from the Dutch oven, I walked to the water again and saw Skye just beyond a giant boulder where the river bent. He was standing in the water up to his waist, casting into an eddy. The sun caught his line in the air and made it shine like a golden string snapping in a nothingness of blue. He was an artist with the rod, a conductor with his wand. I watched him hook a trout and let it run, then I hurried back to the camp before he looked my way.

Silly. Why did I care? I would be with him all week no matter what. And our talk had been so brief, so small—so why had it turned me so far, so fast?

I hadn't noticed Shelby by the fire, looking clean and made-up as ever, as if she hadn't even slept—hair perfect, as usual. She was reading a novel. Wyatt was still in his tent, snoring, even though it must have been seven or eight in the morning. I wasn't sure without my phone.

"What are you reading?" I asked Shelby.

"You'll just make fun of it. Skye already did, so don't worry. I'm trying to get a bunch in before Wyatt wakes up."

"Hey, no judgment here. Romance novels can be fun sometimes," I said.

"Yeah?"

Shelby looked my way as if I'd just informed her that she could live the life she wanted to and not worry about it. I wondered why she was so tightly wound up about what other people thought of her, being as popular as she was. At the same time, maybe I was more like her than I cared to admit. She smiled and went back to her book.

"Although, I have to ask," I said, spooning in some more eggs and sitting across the fire from Shelby, "what is it about those books that keeps you going back for more?"

"I guess I expect something grand at the finish. And even though I expect it, it still happens. Every time. You'd think that would make it boring, right?"

"No. It's nice to go into something knowing where you'll come out. I can't say as much for these eggs. Or candy corn. Every time I pick them up, I expect a grand finish, but I know better by now. Or at least, I should."

She smiled and went back to the pages as I walked to toss my empty breakfast plate. Wyatt finally shuffled into camp and poured himself some orange juice. I shuddered. Whenever I saw "made from concentrate" on a bottle, I wanted to throw up and place the bottle directly in the trash. Give me the real thing.

"How much time do I have?" said Wyatt.

"Nash said we have an hour or so before we get going," said Shelby.

"Where is Nash?" I said.

Shelby pointed her book upstream to where the boat was

sitting. Next to it, I saw Nash in a yoga pose, his ponytail dangling over his shoulder, one leg in the air and the other planted. Then he rotated, his face to the sun, his shoulders near his knees, his legs set in a deep squat. He was a slim man, what Grandpa might call, "Thin as wallpaper and taut as a fiddle string."

"That guy . . ." I said.

"Yep," said Shelby, before I could finish my sentence.

I was glad Shelby seemed to be on my side, even for something so little. It was odd thinking of myself as someone like Shelby, someone Skye would talk to and want to know. I couldn't reconcile the idea with what I saw when I looked in a mirror and what I saw when I looked at how pretty Shelby was.

Nash changed his yoga pose, putting his body on the sand, facedown, and resting with his palms near his chest. Then, he rose and walked back to camp, brushing the sand from his tank top and swim trunks.

"Morning. Glad everybody is awake," said Nash.

"Did you lose something near the boat?" said Wyatt.

"I was partaking in my morning Hindu yogic chakras and Zen koans—riddles to keep the brain humming. I like to start the day with stimulation and balance. It helps keep my mind sharp."

"Sounds interesting," said Wyatt.

Nash went straight to packing up camp, and in less than an hour, we were all lined up next to the boat wearing our PFDs, or "personal flotation devices." We all looked like giant marshmallows, just with water-wicking jackets on. Nash wore one as well. His face looked weary in the stark morning light. My mind was awash with half-words and partial phrases to describe his look, but it all funneled back to that one word: weary.

"Okay, folks," he said, standing on the raft and looking down at us. "We put in yesterday, but it was a slow and steady hump to this campsite, and we had just about zero rapids, so I didn't go over specifics."

I felt a dark bloom in my stomach, knowing it was my anger that changed his plans.

"Probably should have even then, considering what happened to our muffins last night," he said.

Shelby blanched, just as Wyatt spoke up. "Nice work, guys. Nash mentioned bear country, but you weren't listening. Too busy on your phone or touching your robot leg."

"Lay off, man," said Skye.

Wyatt and Skye locked stares, but turned back to Nash when he started up again.

"My fault, not yours," said Nash. "Food always stays on the boat. I just got lazy. Now, we don't have cake mixes, salt and pepper, bread, granola bars, chips, and a lot of other stuff for meals. But we have enough to get by. Just don't be angry about eating meat and cheese for breakfast, lunch, and dinner.

"Anyway, listen up. The river gorge is over seven thousand feet in places. That's about fifty Niagara Falls–worth of drop. It's the deepest river gorge on the planet, not just in the US. Pay attention—this could be life or death—keep that PFD on at all times. It is your main safety device. Listen to me throughout the day, do everything I say. I am experienced and know how to read the water, but I still need you to tell me about obstacles you see coming our way. Now, two choices if you get thrown from the boat—"

"Excuse me," said Shelby, raising her hand, "but I thought this was, like, a river float. I thought we would be in the raft the whole time."

"That's the goal," said Nash. "But just in case you fall out, swim to the boat and we'll pull you back in. If you're far from the boat, you may have to swim through some rapids first. If that happens, float on your back and keep your feet downstream. Hold your breath as the waves break over you. Push off rocks and other obstacles with your feet. Don't use your head."

Wyatt laughed, the sound lodged deep in his throat. It was like an engine backfiring too—as soon as we heard it, everyone looked to see what was making that odd noise. I couldn't judge Wyatt for it, as I had what Grandpa called a "four-alarm laugh."

"Skye knows how to hit things with his head. The whole soccer team—that's what they do. They even practice that crap."

"Maybe you should try out for the team this year, Wyatt," said Skye.

Wyatt went quiet, hugged his arms around his PFD, and stared at Nash with his chin up, without looking anywhere else.

"Pay attention," Nash said, resuming his lecture. "You can also swim to an eddy or the shore if you can't make it to the boat. In a rescue situation, leave the gear and save the people. You'd think I wouldn't have to mention it, but people are attached to their belongings."

Wyatt tilted his head at Shelby, who was scrolling on her phone. "You hear that?"

"Shut up," she said.

Nash continued, "Don't worry about *things*, focus on the *people*. Careful with the paddle as well. Everyone here, I assume, wants to keep their teeth. If you're tossed from the boat, try to hold onto the paddle and use it to get back in. If you can't hold on, don't worry. It's a *thing*, so ditch it and swim to the shore or the boat. There are extra paddles tied to the bottom of this rig. Just make sure you get back to us in one piece."

He stopped to get a drink of water. Shelby looked panicked. Wyatt was as calm as the morning, like a soft breeze in the pines, and Skye shifted uncomfortably next to me, standing and resting his back against a boulder near the shore. He touched his leg and stared up into the sky, ignoring Nash.

"At all costs, avoid being swept under a log or strainer. If you find yourself on your way to one, flip over and swim like hell. If we encounter a strainer situation, I will toss this your way."

He held up something that looked like a rucksack with a loop attached.

"Reach for this, kick hard, and try to get over the strainer so it can't suck you under. If you go under, there is extreme danger and a likelihood that you will not get out. Ditch your life jacket. That sounds counterintuitive, but it may be what has you snagged. Sometimes you can pop out the other end. More often than not, though, you will get stuck below."

Nash looked at me when he finished. I was feeling the clips on my life jacket and imagining what I would do if confronted with that situation. I'd rehearsed that death-trap scenario hundreds of times over the last two years, even though I never planned on rafting again in my life. Fishing, sure, but not rafting.

What was that in Nash's eyes? Empathy? Repentance? Anger? I couldn't tell. I just knew he'd meant that last part for me, to remind me that he knew what he was doing on the river, but that sometimes the river still wins. Nature always wins, right?

"If we hit a rock," Nash continued, "I'll yell 'high side,' and you'll all need to jump to the side of the raft nearest the rock before water gathers on the upstream side or we will wrap around the obstacle. Remember, stay hydrated and put on sunscreen. Drink only properly treated water. All the first aid gear is right here." He kicked a metal box in the raft next to his seat. "We'll be traveling close to eighty miles a day. We need to refill water at a spring tomorrow, but we're set until then. We'll restock at camp three, where Thatcher and Sawyer will meet us with more food and more, well, everything.

"We'll finish up Friday as the Snake connects to the Lower Salmon. This is an oar-rigged boat, so I'll be rowing, and you'll be enjoying this gorgeous canyon and the karma floating in the wind and the way the gods have seen fit to bless you with such a perfect day."

None of us said anything, and an awkward silence fell. Nash cleared his throat. "Remember, if something wild happens, try to get to shore. I'm a professional, so it likely won't. Any questions?"

Shelby's face said *Several*, but she didn't respond. She was too busy filming every word on her phone.

"That reminds me," said Nash, smiling at Shelby. "No phones. Turn them off, and put them in the dry-bag. Here."

"What if it's waterproof to a certain extent?" said Shelby.

"What kind of extent?" said Skye.

"Five feet. For over thirty minutes."

"Well, this is North America's deepest river, but if you don't care about losing your phone, go ahead and hang onto it," said Nash.

Shelby gave Nash a contemptuous look. "It's annoying not to have it, is all."

"This will be good for you guys," said Nash. "Enjoy the real thing. Live, in action."

"Right," said Shelby. "So good."

"Ah, Shelby, you're growing up so much, and it's only our second day!" said Wyatt, holding his hands together in a mocking prayer gesture. "I'm so proud of you."

"I hope you get thrown from the boat," she said.

"Would you rescue me?" asked Wyatt.

"No."

"What if Skye falls out?"

"Still no."

"Hear that, Skye?" said Wyatt. "She's not that into you. Looks like you should have gone with the horseback-riding group to find a girlfriend."

"Bet you wanted to go with that group too. Would have given you a chance to wear your tight Wranglers in front of everyone," said Skye.

"Don't say that," said Wyatt.

"Why? Is denim your soft spot, cowboy? Can't ride the rodeo circuit without the right pair of jeans?"

"I said shut it, Skye."

"Sure thing, pardner."

Wyatt leaped from his position and drove his shoulder right into Skye's stomach. He lifted Skye off the ground and tackled him into the sand, and then pushed Skye's face under the water. He leaned back to avoid Skye's thrashing hands.

Nash yanked Wyatt off Skye, while Shelby and I stood back, holding tightly to our PFDs, unsure of what to do or say or think.

"What is wrong with you two?" said Nash.

Skye blew water from his nose and rubbed his eyes, coughing. "Maniac was trying to drown me!"

"A few inches of water, man. You'll be okay," said Wyatt, smirking.

Nash shook him by his PFD. "Wyatt? What was that?"

"What's the matter, Skye? Can't stand on your own two feet anymore?"

Skye cursed and lunged for Wyatt, his hands curled into fists.

Nash directed the two to separate spots on the raft. He then tossed a yellow bag to Shelby, and Shelby put her phone in. Everybody else must have left their phone packed back in the van like I had.

We hopped into the boat, and Nash talked to us about keeping our feet covered at all times and how to avoid getting our shoes tangled in any rope or rescue bags. That made me think of Skye and his leg. I turned to watch him readjust his prosthetic.

"Not gonna take it off for the ride?" said Shelby.

"I need the balance. Besides, these things are sturdy."

"I could tell," said Wyatt. "Really helps with your center of gravity."

"That's enough, guys," said Nash.

He fastened everything down and pushed us away from the shore, and we began our journey for that day. I watched Skye touch his prosthetic numerous times, looking at it in the morning light as if he wanted to rip it off and throw it away.

I looked into the water at stones that resembled dinosaur eggs shimmering beneath a filtered, blue light. I relished the moment. I caught glances of the gleaming scales of fish at various turns.

Immediately, I felt the heft and weight and pull and strength of the willful current, of the water flowing beneath us, and the way it pushed against what seemed like an incredibly flimsy, floating death trap.

I'd forgotten how small I felt when confronted by water, and this trip only served to increase that fear, that hopeless feeling. We moved up and down with each trough, with each wave. The heat of the morning pressed down upon us. A blanket of green rose from the surrounding stretches of land.

Nash really was skilled with the oars. His arms pivoted, dipped, swayed and stuck when they needed to, each arm rotating at a different speed and angle, depending on the bend of the river and the speed of the water. He looked like he was in his element, which made me question how he could have failed my mother the way he had.

"Any of you remember the story of Echo?" Nash said, noticing we were a quiet bunch as we started the day, particularly Wyatt and Skye.

"I remember Wyatt's snoring echoing last night," said Shelby.

"*That's* what you remember? Not the bear?" said Wyatt.

"*Echo!*" Skye shouted, and we all heard a faint return. He smiled at me, but only got a half attempt in return. Maybe I was being too hard on him. He was just trying to get to know me, maybe, right?

"Exactly," said Nash. "Echo was cursed to only repeat the last word said to her."

"It was a girl?" asked Skye.

"It's not always about a man," said Shelby. "I know that's hard for you guys to understand."

Nash continued, "She was originally set up as a spy for Zeus, because Zeus was messing around with all the wood nymphs."

"Dirty Zeus," said Wyatt. "And yet, he gets all the press. What a jerk."

"Well, Hera found out, and you guessed it: she cursed Echo. Echo fell in love with Narcissus, but she couldn't say anything. So, of course, Narcissus fell in love with himself," said Nash.

"Hear that, Shelby? I thought you and Skye might be the only two left of that kind," said Wyatt.

"Seriously, Wyatt. My face. Eat it," said Shelby.

"Soon enough I'm gonna take you up on that," he said. "And then what will we do?"

"Did you know Hera was the one who named the Milky Way?" I said, hoping to shift the momentum of the conversation, to cut up the tension.

"Really?" said Skye.

"Yeah. My mom told me that Hera said it looked like spilled milk."

"It totally does," said Shelby.

"Yeah. I like that," said Wyatt.

The mountains were splashed with color. The river was bright. I couldn't reconcile the beauty of the landscape with the site of my greatest loss.

Skye leaned out and almost fell into the water reaching for a small fly, trying to cup the bug in his hand.

"Different bugs hatch at different times of the year," Nash said, spying Skye.

"Obvious," I said. "It's not like all mammals give birth during the same month each year."

Nash maneuvered the boat, and light pooled in the pockets of water, throwing little skittering shadows across the river.

"I wish I could get all this on my phone," said Shelby. "This would be gold for my followers."

"Your followers like Greek mythology?" said Wyatt.

"My followers like outdoorsy stuff sometimes. Variety. I don't, but I'll do it if it means getting a few more likes and a few more followers."

"Why do you care so much about how many people follow you?" said Wyatt.

She shrugged. "It's just nice to have a community."

"But it's not like they know you, right? They scroll past and maybe click a like, but then they move on without another thought."

"Maybe. But I like it," she said.

"Yeah. I'm wondering *why*," said Wyatt.

"I don't know. Sometimes I wear a plaid shirt and just step outside my house to get the Tetons in the shot behind me. No one needs to know that I'm wearing slippers and freezing and planning to go right back to bed."

"So you fake it?" asked Wyatt.

"I guess. Sometimes. But I've built a persona that I need to keep up."

"Why?"

"Leave her alone, Wyatt," said Skye.

"What, I can't ask questions?" said Wyatt.

"If you look to your left," said Nash, cutting off the conversation between Wyatt and Shelby and Skye, "you'll see pictographs in the distance. They were carved by the Native Americans of this area who used to run those high ridges. Some artifacts date back eleven thousand years. Shoshone-Bannock, Northern Paiute, and Cayuse Indians used to roam these parts. Lewis and Clark came near this place in 1806."

We were all in board shorts with sandals fit for the water; Shelby and I had on one-piece bathing suits under our shorts. Wyatt had his hair in a bun, and mine was still under my cap. Shelby's hair looked effortless and perfect as usual. Skye was wearing a baseball cap and leaning back onto the side of the boat. He looked up into the sun, his face squinted, his eyes slits in the light.

The way the sun hit the water in that moment was near abstract, like I was looking at a giant printout or a page in an outdoor magazine.

"So, you guys would have been happier climbing or fishing?" I said, hoping to lighten the mood. "You had a fifty percent chance of going on a trip with something you enjoy, I guess. Probability."

"Probability not," said Wyatt.

"I am with something I enjoy," said Skye on the heels of my comment.

I looked away and didn't let him see my smile.

"So cute, Skye," said Wyatt.

"Your man-bun is what's cute, Wyatt," said Skye.

"Thanks. Glad somebody noticed," said Wyatt, pushing his hand against the bun and making it bob. "You know, you go to bed after using some dry shampoo and combing through it a hundred times, wondering if anybody will ever notice how much work you put into it, and then, just like that, somebody notices. Just like that. Thanks, bud."

"Okay, gear up," Nash said. "River left, people. High flow this year, so get ready. This isn't a riffle; this is the real thing. We got a hole here, and a boulder garden near the end of this feature. Hang on. Here we go!"

Just then, the raft dipped and bucked like the unbroken paint in Wyatt's backyard; the horse was always knocking the fencing and neighing in the night. I fell forward and held onto the rope on the side, even though Nash had warned against that. On the next wave, Skye slipped and fell into the hole where our feet were, and then he jumped back up so he could ride the edge for the duration of the feature.

The boat surged from the swells, and Shelby started yelling and holding onto her head. Wyatt grinned as the rapids propelled his body a foot up from the boat, only to land right back where he started. The water sprayed us with every dip and turn, soaking our faces and bodies. I peeked over the edge of the raft to see the pines blurring past as sprays of water misted my face.

Nash flexed in the sunlight, his body seemingly made of oars, his focus set on navigating this first set of rapids. I saw him eye the line and see it through. I knew enough about rafting that I could see the same line, mark the same features.

As we hit the boulder garden, we knocked into two rocks, but nothing substantial. We were all soaked by the time we hit the quiet waters below. Wyatt was laughing, and Shelby started in as well. The rapids hadn't lasted long, but each moment in the white blitz of water had seemed like an impossibly long time.

"This. Is. *Awesome*," said Wyatt.

"Wow," said Shelby, holding Wyatt's leg as she got back up to her place on the edge of the raft.

"Lost your shoe?" I said, eyeing Skye. I may have had my eye more on his arms, but I wasn't going to say that.

"Something like that," he said. "Just a little slip."

He must have noticed us staring at his prosthetic, because he adjusted in his spot and then spoke. "You all just wish you had a leg up on me."

"Just wait until we climb," said Wyatt. "Should we climb tomorrow morning before we get on the water, Skye? I saw you tying those knots."

"That's okay, man."

"Scared of heights?" asked Wyatt.

"Something like that."

We'd spoken to Nash about climbing, and he'd agreed to let us climb at camp if we wanted. We were also planning on climbing again on the final day after we pulled out of the river, because then we'd have extra guides to help. It all had to be easy climbs—he didn't want to risk anything.

"Everyone okay?" said Nash.

All smiles. He looked around the boat, and I could tell he was in his element. He smiled back, and I saw the living waters in his face, the rock gardens in his brain, the way his mind maundered just like the river.

There was an echo of the river in his soul, and he let it show. In that moment, I felt forgiveness lurching from my insides, trying to escape my tight grasp. I felt a lightness enter my chest as I imagined letting the past go. But I couldn't. Because in that moment, I also saw the strainer, and I remembered staring at it months after she was gone, my fly-rod in hand, my head bent. I felt the ring on my chest.

"Nothing better in life than that ride," he said. "With daily water levels changing at the dam, you can never really plan for that first one. Those were the Wild Sheep Rapids."

"Very wild," said Shelby.

I realized I was still clenching my teeth and the muscles in my back in anticipation of the next maw of water, the next dip and rise in the frothy white. The roar of the water was behind us as we eased into softer, calmer currents, the rapids in the background still shouting into the morning sky.

We worked through Granite Rapids and Three Creek Rapids before stopping for lunch. By then it was late afternoon, and everyone was sore from tensing our way down the river. But we were still all smiles.

We dried off on a sandbar as Nash pulled the cooler ashore

into the shade of the pines. Rock features exploded in every direction, the geometry of the land a stark contrast to the rapidly changing shapes of the water. Honestly, I was just glad to rest on the sand and let everything else stop moving for a moment. I soaked up the warmth of the sun, listening to the faint roar of the water set against the insular quiet of the sandbar.

Nash let us relax as he prepped lunch. The four of us stared into the sky, arms over eyes, or squinting. I was starting to doze off, when Nash shouted for us to come grab some food.

"Do you think it can be any worse than breakfast?" said Shelby.

A few options popped up before my face, and I scrolled through them in my mind.

1. *It's probably worse. Go in expecting that, and you might be surprised.*
2. *Of course. Everything in life is downhill, and if we started with mediocre barbecued chicken, what do you think is next?*
3. *Yes. I saw him preparing horsemeat and fish skins, and I know for a fact he doesn't wash his hands.*
4. *We're having a late night and some Pepto if it's anything like breakfast.*

Turns out it was option number 1. It was just deli meat and cheese slices, but it was better than any of us expected. Or maybe we were just hungry after a long morning. Probably both. He mentioned at lunch, again, how the other members of his outfit would meet us on day three with new supplies, more food, and a fully setup campsite. That sounded wonderful in the wake of so much movement and the loss of all our dry goods.

Skye looked my way a couple times during lunch, but I didn't give him the time to see that I knew I was overreacting to an innocent advance. But I still felt something was off about his reasoning for flirting with me instead of Shelby, and I needed to process it before letting him in. Right?

After lunch, Nash finished reloading the raft and then stepped back to the small circle we'd created around a flat rock where our drinks rested.

"Can I get my phone out for a minute?" said Shelby.

"Let's keep it in the dry-bag for now. You can this evening." Nash paused. "You know, I take all my clients to this spot on the first full day."

He said it like we should congratulate him or something, like he'd done something amazing by getting us to the same spot every other tour group had been to.

"Why?" said Wyatt, breaking the awkward pause. Wyatt—playing the kind soul. Was that normal for him? I couldn't tell. Nobody could.

"Come with me."

We all hesitated, and Nash probably noticed, because he repeated himself.

"Come on. It won't take too long."

We all stood and gathered our trash in a bag and stepped around a large outcropping of chokecherry shrubs. In the distance, birds shouted at the sky or maybe each other. I couldn't see them. Probably out for their own lunch, diving for a trout twisting in the cool waters. We stopped next to a giant cotton-wood tree and saw a large pile of stones on the ground.

"Everybody grab a stone and place it on this pile," said Nash.

"Why?" I said.

"In memory of Joyce Lutz."

I stopped and stared at Nash. He didn't flinch. He looked sincere. The others briefly looked at me before picking up a stone.

"There's an old Scottish blessing," said Nash, "'I'll put a stone on your stone.'"

"Doesn't sound like it means much," I said.

"Think about it. If we want a true memorial, that needs to happen."

"I'm going to find a rock," I said, turning to step beyond the cottonwood tree and the chokecherry shrubs.

I didn't mean to cry. I didn't want to cry. I didn't have it in my mind to ever be found crying again by anybody, anywhere, at any time. But tears poured from my eyes. A torrent. I stifled the sobs as best I could, but then I saw Wyatt with his stone. He didn't say a word. He just walked over to my spot on the sand, sat next to me, and pulled me into him. The blast radius of my mother's life seemed to be much larger than I ever imagined.

Wyatt stood moments later and walked to the pile without a word. I shook my head, my hair falling into my eyes. My hands clenched into fists.

Eventually, I summoned the courage to walk back to that pile, that monument, and picked out a stone. Not without my doubts, of course. Had Nash known he was picking the weakest line in the river? Had he asked Joyce for her help because he wanted to reunite, or because he felt incompetent on the water without her? Did he really take every group here, or was this just a cairn marking a walking path and Nash was putting on a show for me?

Still holding my stone, I saw Nash and Shelby standing next to the shrubs, looking for rocks. His skin looked weathered in the harsh light, his eyes deeper in his face, his chest a little more concave, his arms heavier, his shoulders bent.

"It's not the size of the pile, Indie," he said to me. "It's what it represents."

I saw Shelby messing with her hair again and felt heat rise to my face.

"Seriously, Shelby? Can you just think about somebody else for two seconds? Can you not just put a stone on there and think about my mother instead of your freaking hair?"

Her face went white, and she slinked behind the shrubs. Nobody said anything.

"You take every group here, or was the pile already there?" I said to Nash. "You putting this on just for me?"

"You don't think that moment haunts me every day, Indie?"

He took a few steps closer. The others were probably waiting around the corner, near the cottonwood and the rock pile.

"Then why didn't you quit the river? Why are you still guiding at, what—fifty?"

"It's all I know. It's all I've ever known. I don't have an education like your mother. I couldn't afford it."

"There are other jobs," I said.

"But I can't afford not to be here. Oddly enough, the only

thing that takes my mind off it is when I know I have to look out for others. That's it."

"That's it."

"I guess I figured if I got enough lives through this canyon here, I could somehow trick karma into letting me have another shot at it all," he said.

"At what?"

"At life! At not feeling this boulder of guilt in my stomach every morning and every night and every moment in between. I know she was your mother, but you should remember she was also my *friend*. I don't expect you to forgive me, Indie, but I do expect you to put a stone on that pile and know that it means a lot more to me than a pile of rocks."

"Then tell me how it really happened. Some people said she fell out. Others said she was trying to save someone. That doesn't make sense. No guide would do that. You said as much, at the funeral. Grandpa is inclined to believe you, but I'm not so sure," I said.

"I told your grandpa the truth."

"Then say it to me again," I said.

He wiped sweat from his forehead and adjusted his bandana, a yellow one with bright birds all over it. A flotilla of clouds sailed by at a quick clip in the blue-white distance.

"It was a strainer, like I said. Her boat was right behind mine. Oar-rigged. We each had our own crew. I went through the boulder garden first, and it was my job to stick with the kid who fell out. We both saw the strainer, but your mother was quicker and got her throw bag in the water. But in the process, another client slipped and knocked her into the water. And I hesitated. And that's all it took to be too late."

"I don't remember that in the papers."

"Because they only ever print part of the story. The whole story is always bigger. I don't like to remember it either," he said.

"So, she was doing something you wouldn't—or couldn't?"

"I just hesitated, is all. A kid fell out and your mother saw the strainer and tossed the bag first. And then she was un-lucky. That's all it was. She fell out and followed that kid to the strainer. We were only able to save the kid because she was able to shift his line and keep him back. Just by a second, but that was enough. For him. She couldn't change her own path at that point.

"She was always better at reading a line than me. She'd already set her boat up to get out clean, so they did. Just not her. But those are not excuses, Indie," said Nash. "I should've thrown the bag out to the kid first. And to her. But I hesitated, and when I reached for it—and her—she was already under."

"Okay," I said, after what felt like an entire week of silence.

"Okay?"

"Okay. That sounds like her," I said, feeling the weight of forgiveness I'd kept coiled inside. "She'd throw that thing with-out hesitation, every time. No matter what. And yeah, I would have hesitated as well. But you shouldn't have. That was your job. Your line—your client. But, okay."

He seemed surprised by my response and how I walked with him back to the pile, how I let the moment go, how I offered some hope of a release on some hold I never thought I had. I wasn't trying to release him—and I didn't—but I was trying to allow myself to unclench my fists around the forgiveness I knew I needed to give. And in that moment, I remembered Grandpa talking to me about catch and release, and I understood what he meant. But I wasn't ready to crush the barb and let it go. I couldn't.

I leaned against an outcropping, stepping out of the heat and hot beams overhead, and considered that I'd built a wall between me and the whole truth, the whole story, and that I'd forced the blame on another. I'd rested in the shadows of that wall for two years and let my life move on without considering that Nash was on the other side of that wall with the rest of the story, and he'd been bearing it alone. He had his own weight to carry without adding my heaviness to it.

But I wasn't ready to give forgiveness. Not fully. Not in that moment, though that monument did a lot in teaching me not just what Nash wanted to do to remember, but the weight of what he was holding onto. All those stones. My stone on his.

As I walked around to the pile where the others waited with him, he gave me a half-smile.

Shelby was there with her rock, looking sheepish. It's not like in the movies where two actors can step away from another character and speak as loud as they want and the audience knows the other character won't hear it or isn't supposed to. This was real life, and I knew they'd all heard our conversation. I felt the heat in my neck and face as I saw them with their stones in hand.

"I bring everyone here to remind them of the power of the river right behind you," said Nash. "It won't take any thought for a life, so don't give it a reason to. It's bigger than all of us, and it moves with more power than you know."

I guess I was expecting some overdone stage production, something shot through with far too much sentimentality, but Nash just said Mom's name as he placed his stone. I placed my rock on the pile, and the rest followed. Did I hate Nash for not saving Mom, for not throwing first, or myself for not agreeing to go? Maybe I could have saved her. Or maybe I would've been in the seat of the person who slipped and knocked Mom overboard.

Their stones on my stone.

I walked to the raft before Nash could ask me anything else, or say something that might spark some form of relief or absolution. That wasn't mine to give, at least not that afternoon. As I sat near the raft waiting for the others, something my mother always said, something Grandpa had mentioned to me the day I left, filled my mind: "Everything and everyone deserves to be sought after and known." I guess Nash was part of everyone, right? But what happens when everybody hoards secrets? How is it possible to get to know them, truly?

I rolled the red sand through my fingers, watching it sparkle as it rained down on my tanned legs and worked its way into my sandals. Shelby came around the corner and looked hesitant, but continued my way. The others followed, and Skye said Nash was busy cleaning up lunch. I felt self-conscious around Shelby, particularly after my earlier comment. I meant it, but I could have said it better. Isn't that always the case?

Nobody spoke, and I felt I had to fill the silence. I always felt that way, though, like I needed to act as a bridge from one thing to the next so things didn't quiet down to the point that I'd be left with the screaming in my head. I liked to keep myself preoccupied with, well, anything but my own thoughts and who I was, who I wanted to be, who I might turn out as. The works.

"Mars has finer dust and sand than anything on Earth," I said. "That's what my mom told me. That's why they have to be careful about what they send up there. Oh, and did you know NASA lost a $125-million rover because they did the math wrong?"

"Sounds about right," said Wyatt. "Math is the worst."

"It's actually pretty cool," I said. I immediately felt heat enter my cheeks, and I tried to take the comment back. "I mean, it's alright sometimes to learn about stuff, if you're bored. Hey, my mom was a teacher, so I kind of had to learn about it, right?"

"Why do you do that?" asked Skye.

"Do what?" I said.

"Pretend like you're not smart. Or get embarrassed about knowing things. Or say you only know something because of your mother. Why do you pretend you're not clever?"

"Because I'm not," I said.

"Yes, you are," said Wyatt.

"Yep," said Shelby.

"Did you read Wixom's packet?" asked Skye.

"Yeah. And I read articles by all the people she mentioned. It was fascinating."

"Good. Own it," said Skye.

I was sure my face was the color of the sand at our feet.

"I'm already made fun of for other stuff, though. Why add to the list?" I said.

"It won't make it worse," said Wyatt. "It will shut those people down. Show them you're smarter. Not to hurt them, but to—I don't know—make yourself seen."

"So I can be just like them?" I said.

"What? What do you mean?" asked Skye.

"Why do they bully in the first place? They probably have to pretend they're not clever at home around their parents, who don't really know them or appreciate them. Just like every teenager." I looked at Skye before finishing. "Or they pretend around their friends for the same reason."

"Get back to the math part," said Wyatt.

I held Skye's gaze for a beat, then turned to Wyatt. "One lab used the metric system of millimeters and sent their data to another lab that used the English system of inches."

"That's an expensive mistake," said Skye.

"We all do that, though," I said. "Right? Math can account for almost everything, but we use the wrong equation and then we're screwed. I mean, Mom used all those laws of physics in class and all that math she always talked about. And yet we don't have math for a person."

"Judgy math," said Shelby. "We've got plenty of that."

"Sounds right," said Wyatt. "Right, Skye?"

Nash emerged around the corner, and we all climbed into the raft. I found myself watching the water, thinking about the math behind each wave, each ripple, each rock and its position in the river. I thought of Newton's third law of motion and wondered if I'd made the right moves with this odd group—the right actions.

There was a buzzing everywhere. The afternoon hatch of bugs blanketed the water in the quieter stretches, adding music to that winding mosaic of blue. But I could only feel the buzzing in my chest as Nash stepped back into the raft and took the oars in hand.

SIX

Four-letter word for a "spike in adrenaline"? *Rush*. That was the word bobbing in my mind when we hit our last set of rapids that first day. We swayed to every move in the water like it was a waltz, but we had no control, no lead, no idea if it would end nicely or turn into some maniacal samba or demented foxtrot before leaving us to spin a solo pirouette at center stage.

Good thing Nash knew what he was doing. Well, at least up to that point. Because when I say *that point*, I mean the moment it all went sideways. Or at least two people went sideways.

We had just entered the Lower Bernard Creek Rapids. The water was crimped in the late afternoon light, throwing spangled lines against the canyon walls. I don't remember any breeze or seeing anything but the light on the bottom of the raft that made it look like it was covered in blue-and-black oil slicks.

I don't remember Nash yelling "High side!" but Wyatt said later that Nash yelled it three times. I must have responded without realizing it, and so did Wyatt. Shelby always had to be the first one in the boat, so it was perhaps fitting that she was the first one out. Skye came right after her into the shifting tide, the raging white-water spin cycle.

When Skye emerged from the water, Nash had us positioned to pull him back in. My sunglasses and hat had gone overboard, leaving me half-blinded by the sunlight off the water. I saw Skye half-inhaling water soup for a second lunch, and I saw the raft bumping off a boulder right before another swell caught Shelby and threw her back under the water. This happened so many times, I worried she might be stuck in a whirlpool of some sort.

Then, just like that, the river switched from "spin cycle" to "all done." The waters calmed, and Skye emerged, still coughing up the river.

"Come on in," he sputtered. "The water's fine."

Shelby floated behind the raft, and Nash leaned over and checked to make sure she was okay. I couldn't see her from where I was sitting, but we asked Nash if we could join Skye in the calm water, and he said that would be fine, since we would be pulling out there anyway.

We were all soaked already, so it seemed like a good idea. Wyatt and I jumped in. Cool relief sank into my chest as I breathed in, my back to the water, my face to the sky, letting the life vest carry me slowly away from the whipped tops of the rapids. I felt the heat on my face and sat up, trying not to fall too far forward. With the PFD on, I was like a human buoy set adrift.

I saw Wyatt paddling his way to the shore. Skye was already there. Nash guided the boat in and pulled it onto the sand. The way Nash had handled those rapids made me feel more confident in his abilities. He'd been aware of everybody at every moment. Even now, he was laughing with Skye about the spill and making sure he was okay.

I still couldn't read Nash. And that's why I still couldn't offer him any escape from his guilt. No big deal, because I also couldn't offer myself any escape from my own guilt.

Then Shelby emerged from the water ten feet from me. She'd been holding onto the other side of the raft on the far side of the river, staying between the boat and the shore until we pulled into the sandbar. I saw her bobbing up and down, her hands white from her death grip on the neckline of her PFD as she released the guideline on the raft.

I could never figure out why we grab the rope for safety when we feel fear while climbing or hold onto the life vest when we fear drowning. Better to simply grab onto the wall or start swimming. It would be like holding a bag of flour in our hands when hungry, hoping it will turn into food.

But when I saw Shelby, I blinked in shock and surprise. Shelby was completely bald. *Bald.* Four-letter word for "not needing a comb," for "tires with no tread left," for "(blank)-faced lie." The crossword clues shot through my brain as I rubbed water from my eyes. I squinted against the reflecting sun to make sure I was seeing things correctly. I was.

The sun was not just reflecting off the water, but off Shelby's head. She was hairless, smooth, stark, unadorned. "Undisguised" was the word stuck in my mind as I saw water wick from her head.

I collapsed onto the sand next to Shelby, my shoulder against hers as we stared into the sky, both of us still attempting to fully catch our breath. I didn't know what to say about her baldness, so I said nothing.

Wyatt and Skye were on either side of us, resting on their backs.

Nash waded into the water, his ponytail like a silver snake hanging off his shoulder, dripping water onto his twisted and waterlogged tank top as he dunked himself in and then re-emerged. He joined us on the sand with a grin.

"Congratulations on your first dip, guys. Next time we'll be quicker about getting to the high side, right?" he said, eyeing Skye and Shelby. "Nice work on keeping those feet downriver and making your way to the shore, though. Did you notice that, Wyatt and Indie? That was really great work."

Nash grabbed some small towels and threw them to us, then rolled his ponytail in his hands like it was a piece of dough. "You guys dry off, and I'll start setting up camp for the evening." He headed down the sand, humming to himself.

Shelby sighed loudly. "Say it."

"Say what?" I asked. "That I'm glad you and Skye are alive? Because I am. Or that I'm sorry about earlier? Because I am. I shouldn't have said what I said."

"I'm bald."

"Didn't even notice," said Skye.

"Right," said Shelby.

"I noticed," said Wyatt. "But I have to say, you pull it off."

Shelby rolled her eyes. "You have to say that because of social conventions."

"Or because I mean it," said Wyatt. "I can mean things, too, you know."

"Can you?" said Skye.

"Yes. I can," said Wyatt, laughing.

Skye shook his head. "Shut up, man."

"It's just hilarious, is all," said Wyatt. "And kind of annoying."

"What is?" I said.

"Here's a woman on her high horse—sorry, *dressage* horse—beloved by all Teton High for her looks, and it's not even true."

"Shut up, Wyatt," said Skye.

"No, I mean it's not true that her looks are a lie. That's why I said it was also annoying. Because she still looks beautiful without the wig."

"Oh. Yeah. Well, that's true," said Skye.

Shelby closed her eyes. I wasn't sure if the water coming off the side of her face was salty tears or simply river water.

We all waited for her to say something. For a moment, the only sound was the distant rapids. I felt a shell of ice on my body as a cool breeze whipped past us. I wanted to nestle into the warm sand, away from my soaked position, or maybe change clothes and start a fire to get truly warm and dry. I sat up just as Shelby began to speak.

"It's called *alopecia totalis*. It's an autoimmune disorder."

"Autoimmune?" said Skye.

"When I was five, I started losing my hair. That's why I didn't want to come on this stupid trip. I hate water."

"I think you're a freaking savage," I said.

"Because I hate water?"

"Because you deal with this and you keep going," I said.

"I'm sure you all deal with stuff."

"Just canning peaches at the right time of year," said Wyatt.

"Can you ever be serious, man? Just once?"

I spoke up. "I would probably hide in some corner of my trailer, waiting for hair to grow. I'm not that hard-core."

"Already tried that," she said with a half-smile. "My hair is never going to grow back." She shook her head. "I thought the adhesive was waterproof. I triple-checked. Maybe it was, and the force of the water just took it. Ugh, that was a two-hundred-dollar mixed-color bob."

"You paid two hundred bucks for that?" said Wyatt.

"My parents did," she said. "Surprised you didn't assume that to begin with."

It was quiet for a beat.

"Okay. My secret is out. So, fess up, everybody. Tell us something we don't know. Something nobody else knows about you. Mine is already out in the open. With water on it. And the sun. And bugs," she said, smacking her head.

It was quiet. This time for many beats.

"C'mon, guys. Help me out a little here," she said.

"Okay," said Skye, quietly.

"Okay?" said Shelby.

Silence fell again. For a lot longer.

Then Skye said, "I was driving."

"What?" said Wyatt.

"I was driving the car the night we crashed. Lewis was asleep. Not me."

"Seems like a weird thing to lie about," said Wyatt. "I mean, you were the one who got hurt."

"I know, right?" said Skye. "That's not even the worst part."

"Okay, what's the worst part?" said Shelby.

"I told the police that I started nodding off because we were exhausted. I told Lewis that. I told my parents that."

"And the truth?" I said.

"Truth is, I was checking my phone."

Shelby exhaled hard through her nose and said, "I thought I was the one with the phone issues."

"What was so important that it couldn't wait?" said Wyatt.

"That's the dumb thing," said Skye. "I'd emailed the manager at Teton Valley Lodge about applying to guide fly-fishing tours. I thought he was responding. Either that, or it was an angry text from my dad."

"But isn't that what your dad does?" said Wyatt. "Lead fly-fishing tours?"

"Yeah. That's why I was worried about it. I figured the manager asked my dad about it, and my dad was texting me to ask what the hell I was thinking, putting fishing before my scholarships."

"Scholar*ships*? As in, more than one?" said Wyatt.

"Yeah. Key word being *was*," said Skye.

"Why does it matter if you wanted to fish?" asked Wyatt.

"Because I'm supposed to play soccer. That's always been the plan."

"Whose plan?" I said.

"Exactly," said Wyatt.

Skye was quiet for a minute. "Well, now you know my secret. It's not a big deal. At least it was my own fault I lost my leg." He shifted his weight in the sand.

"I think the application to guide is the bigger secret," I said. "So what was the alert for? On your phone?"

"Whatever," he said, ignoring me. "We'll see what happens. I don't even know if I want to do that anymore."

"Why not?" said Wyatt.

"Whose turn is it now?" said Skye, deflecting again.

"I think that's it," said Wyatt. "We should probably help set up camp."

"That's messed up, guys," said Skye. "C'mon."

"Wyatt's right," I said. "Wouldn't want to seem entitled or lazy."

"You still have to go," said Skye.

"Maybe later," I said.

We all stood up, and Skye and Wyatt took off to set up tents and change clothes. Shelby brushed the sand from her shorts, and I realized I was still staring at her. I hadn't noticed before that her eyebrows were drawn on. They looked so perfect, like the rest of her.

"Wish you had your phone so it could go viral?" she said.

"I don't think that way," I said.

"I do. I wish I didn't. It's okay, though. I get it. It's weird."

"No, you don't get it. I'm staring because I think you look really pretty. I think it's amazing."

She gave me a look heavy with apprehension, but I felt like most of my comment had gotten through to her.

As we set up our tents, I kept thinking of Nash and the food we'd lost to the bear. I wondered how Nash had communicated with his crew to let them know to bring more food to our meet-up the next day, since Nash had said the radio wasn't working.

I knew exactly where it was—partly because Nash kept

looking at it on his shoulder that first day, and, later, at the dry-bag he kept it in while on the raft, but mostly because it called to me, promising me a way out. But I was also starting to want that way out less and less as I got more and more of the people around me. People like Shelby and her unabashed baldness.

Forty minutes later, we were all in the same dry clothes from the night before and sitting next to the fire Nash had started while we were setting up tents.

The most noticeable thing: Shelby was wearing another wig. I didn't feel like I could ask her about it yet, but I nodded and she smiled and we let it go. I was surprised she'd packed one, though, because Thatcher had been adamant about us only taking essentials for two days, and a backup wig didn't seem essential. Well, I guess not to me because that wasn't my life.

The fire moved like a school of red-orange fishes toward the logs, sparks leaping into the higher reaches of the pines that stretched over the campsite and out over the river. Nash looked beaten down by the day, or perhaps it was just his wrinkled features in the firelight.

"We have a lot of fruit for dinner tonight," said Nash. "I'm still looking for some MREs, but I think we lost nearly all of the good dry food. I'm so sorry, team. I have a few more eggs and some cheese for breakfast—leftovers from today's lunch. Or would you prefer to eat them now?"

Nobody spoke. We looked at one another. I think the others were as surprised as I was, and we were all questioning just how great this guide was.

"Okay. Well, we'll save the eggs and cheese for breakfast, I guess."

"How can your radio not work? Don't you plan for the whole no-reception thing?" Wyatt said. Wyatt: always the brave one. Or maybe just the brash one. Maybe just the disrespectful, belligerent one.

Not that he was super brave in mentioning it, but brave in that he was calling out an adult. Yes, we were nearly all adults ourselves, but there was still this odd, almost transparent wall between teenagers and adults that we were afraid to step through or cross over or reach through sometimes.

Wyatt seemed to care very little for that idea, and I think we were all happy he said what we were thinking. Besides, nothing is worse than a group of hangry teenagers sitting by a fire with no internet and no car and no friend's house to escape to.

"The radio is an old one, but I was hoping it would last one more trip. It's my fault. I should have purchased a new one before this journey so I could warn the crew. But, like I said, lots of food will be waiting for us tomorrow. And Thatcher will have the rest of the clothes you packed, and you can switch out for any gear you'd like. If you want a different tent or sleeping bag, he'll have those as well. Plus more fresh water."

"I can take care of dinner," said Skye. "I'm in the mood for some trout."

"Thanks, Mama Bear. Can you bring back some berries, too?" said Wyatt.

"Gross," said Shelby. "I hate fish."

"Well, they may not like you very much either," said Wyatt.

"You'd rather eat eggs again?" Skye said.

"Fine. Do your thing," said Wyatt.

Skye slowly moved to his tent to get his rod. Our makeshift

campsite had a lot of mud but very little open space. It was clearly not a first option for river guides, but I appreciated Nash telling us to call it a day earlier than was probably normal after Shelby and Skye's spill into the river.

We were still close enough to the Lower Bernard Creek Rapids that we could hear the rumbling as they ripped through the canyon just over one hundred yards from our site. A fan of light sat on the ridge of the canyon, and I watched as a bald eagle glided in the air, just sitting there, floating.

Skye returned minutes later, hunching to avoid scraping his face on the pine needles at eye-level next to the tent ring we'd formed—we didn't have as much space to spread out as we'd had the night before. In fact, Nash's tent was within twenty yards of mine, which made me uncomfortable. But at least it might deter bears, right?

"Give me a half hour, and I should have some trout ready. We can have fish and fruit."

"Happy hunting," I said.

"I'm fishing."

"Whatever," I said. "Still. It's not a wand and you're not a princess. The rod can handle an actual cast. Try to let it load like you know what you're doing, and not like you cast this morning."

"You were watching me?"

"Maybe," I said.

Wyatt shook his head, then stood up and headed into the trees. Shelby grabbed her phone and aimed for the shoreline. I wasn't close enough to hear what she was saying, but I figured it was about our awesome spill earlier.

Skye walked to the river's edge and propped his body against a rock and leaned into his cast. It unfolded perfectly over the water like a kite string unspooling in a breeze. He was a master with the rod, and not many things impressed me like seeing someone properly cast a line and effortlessly float a fly for a hook set. Mom cast like that. Like it was part of her DNA.

Skye landed two big trout, and we had just finished preparing them for the fire when Wyatt returned holding what looked like an awful salad in his hands. He walked over to the fish and rubbed the greenery all over them before we set them in the fire to roast.

"Jack by the hedge," said Wyatt.

We all looked around the fire to see if we could see a person, let alone something that might be termed a hedge.

"Not a person," he said. "It's a relative of the cabbage. Tastes like garlic. Trust me."

"Who you calling Mama Bear now, man?" said Skye.

Wyatt shot back, "Whatever. It's good."

We trusted him, and it paid off. Turns out we didn't really need the almost-tastes decent food in the cooler, because Skye and Wyatt were equipped with enough know-how to keep us well-fed, as long as they could cooperate long enough to cook a fish.

"Thanks for the dinner, guys," Shelby said.

"I thought you hated fish," I said.

"Hate's such a strong word, Indie. I dislike fish, I guess. But when you're hungry, almost anything tastes good."

I turned to Skye. "Next time, let me know if you want to learn how to properly float a line in fast-moving waters."

"You'll teach me how to fly-fish?"

"Some things can't be taught. But you can watch me and try to get some insight."

I hadn't spoken to him much that day, and it seemed to bring a great deal of relief into his face when I said that.

What we all knew, but didn't mention, was that Skye's dad was the most famous guide in Victor. Probably the most expert fisherman in Idaho. He was often booked out months before any other guide. He was one of the handful of guides who truly understood the way the river worked, how it moved, how it slept, how it woke and turned its face to the morning sun, and how it hungered with a particular appetite for specific bugs. I imagined Skye also knew the riverbends near our home backwards, forwards, and sideways.

I thought his dad sounded a lot like Grandpa. I've heard fly-fishermen talk about the river the same way others talk about God. Grandpa said the best fishing holes were secrets between him and the Good Lord, and that those spots were saved for the most devout, the most religious.

Grandpa seemed to know what fish were biting at any moment, even if he was sleeping, as if he had dreams of Klinkhammers and Caddis and Red Quill snagging the perfect brown or rainbow trout. Mosquitos and gnats meant more to him than the rest of us. Any flies, really. I often noticed him just letting bugs land on him and watching them intently. He never waved his hand to get rid of the bugs—he just slowed down and looked closer, squinting and talking to himself and the bug under his breath.

"Well, I'm off to meditate," said Nash. "I'll be near my tent if you need me. Be ready for an early start. I'd like to make good headway before lunch. Make sure to drink a lot of water tonight, because it's supposed to be hot tomorrow. We'll get new supplies near Hominy Creek—and more food. But, hey, we saved almost half a bag of marshmallows, as long as you don't mind possible bear breath on them. Thanks for the fish, Skye and Wyatt. Right. G'night, team."

It seemed early for Nash to be heading off to his tent, but he also seemed a bit hangdog, for some reason. It wasn't a big deal, but any lack of professionalism carried a lot more meaning and weight considering my presence and Nash's history with my mom. I knew Nash was feeling the pressure of needing to provide a perfect trip down the Snake River for a few teenagers on nice, sunny, summer days. Then again, maybe he was just tired.

If I'd been a bird at that moment, I would have risen above our camp and looked down on the small, pine-needle-covered paths between bunches of trees and sharp rocks and limbs reaching into the river like fingers. I imagined I'd be able to see our group around the fire like dots around a small sun. Maybe I'd be able to see other outfits with other rafters in boats—some on the shore, some stuck in eddies, some bathing, and some still floating down the river looking for a campsite. Maybe I'd even be able to see a smoke tendril rise up and around a large Fremont poplar tree from our campsite.

But I wasn't a bird. That was ridiculous. I was tired, and

I was tired of thinking about Nash, so I let my attention snap back to the fire and stay with the group.

"I never thought I'd say this, but being with you guys isn't the worst," said Shelby.

"We're not the worst? That's so sweet, Shelbs," said Wyatt. He opened the tied half-bag of marshmallows and put one on a stick.

"Gross. And don't call me Shelbs."

"Shelbs it is," said Skye, nodding for the marshmallow bag.

"Weren't you guys terrified of coming on this trip? I was. I was promised an easy week, but it's never easy when adults say things like that. I hate getting wet," she said, gesturing to her wig. "At least I'll end up with tons of good material for my followers."

"Me too," said Wyatt.

"You have followers?" I asked.

"Well, you wanted a secret," said Wyatt. "Something no-body knows about, right?"

"Yeah," said Skye. "I just never thought you'd share."

"Neither did I. But there you go. That's mine."

"What's yours?" I asked.

"My secret. I have followers. Kind of. I run a blog about art," he said. "Well, it's mostly about the way light is handled in different works of art. Don't tell my dad, or he'll lose it."

"Seriously?" said Skye.

"Yeah. He's pretty small-minded," said Wyatt. "Kind of like you and your buddies."

"That's not fair, Wyatt," said Shelby.

"It's not? Do you even know about what he did, Shelbs? Why don't you tell them about Chisum, Skye?"

Skye breathed out, his shoulders slumping. He looked away from the fire, squinting into the dark. "That wasn't me, man."

"That wasn't you, *man*? I thought you said you rolled with Royal and Chase. That not true anymore, now that you're trying to impress Indie?" asked Wyatt.

"I remember Chisum," said Shelby. "That wasn't your fault, Wyatt."

Wyatt gave a loud mock-laugh. "I know it wasn't my fault. I know *exactly* whose fault it was," he said. "Skye and his buddies basically killed my friend. Isn't that right, Skye? Buddy?"

"I wasn't a part of it, Wyatt," said Skye. He dropped his stick into the fire and let the marshmallow on the end burn. He started tapping his prosthetic again.

"Sure you weren't," Wyatt said.

"I had nothing to do with it," said Skye.

"They're your friends, right?"

"They *were*. They're not anymore. I'm not the same person," said Skye. He threw a rock into the fire.

"So what person were you? What did you do? Too shy to say it now?"

"I didn't know what they were going to do," said Skye quietly.

"Of course you didn't," said Wyatt. "Because your friends are always looking to learn new things, to brush up on editing tech, right? They're always eager to learn and grow for the sake of knowledge, and not to bully, right?"

"I only showed them how to use some things on Lightroom. I didn't know why they needed to know that."

"Right," said Wyatt.

"I swear," Skye said.

Wyatt went on to recount the story, but from an angle I hadn't heard.

Chisum was a kid in our high school who was gay, but hadn't announced it or come out about it or whatever. But rumors are alive—and sometimes vicious. Some kids at school had taken Chisum's photo and made it look like he had the body of Heath Ledger, the guy from *Brokeback Mountain*. In the picture, he was wearing a cowboy hat and standing next to a naked man. A speech bubble above him said, "Why Can't I Quit You?" In our town, those things tended to stick around because of how they portrayed the West and the cowboy code, and how they mocked small towns like Victor and Tetonia.

They were posted all over the school one morning. The principal took them down immediately, but it was too late. That night Chisum shot himself with his dad's Colt revolver in their tack shed. The horses whinnied until his mother found him there, on the floor.

"I'm sorry, Wyatt," said Skye. "I am. I didn't know what they were going to do."

"But they were your friends. That's all I'm saying."

"Not anymore. That's all *I'm* saying."

"What's changed?" asked Wyatt. He threw his burnt marshmallow into the fire and put another one on the stick. I wasn't sure why—maybe just to watch something burn.

"A lot," said Skye.

"Like?"

"Like a lot. I don't even know who my friends are anymore."

"I can make a list," said Wyatt. "I know who they are."

"No. I don't have any."

Wyatt turned his head from the fire, but I didn't think it was because of the smoke.

Skye grabbed the marshmallow bag and shifted in his spot, pushing a log aside to open up a spot for the coals. "I can't play soccer anymore, and my parents don't know what to do because now they can't keep harping on me about scholarships. Like I said."

"How sad," said Wyatt.

"Look, Wyatt, I'm used to letting my parents tell everyone that I'm this amazing soccer player set for a big university and a starting position, so I just smile and nod. But I don't love soccer the way I love other things. That's why I was checking my phone for that email, because I care more about other stuff. But I let my parents say it, because it was easier than standing up to it. Which is basically what happened with Chisum—it was easier for me to just let my friends do what they wanted than ask why or try to stop them. I didn't even know I was doing it. 'There goes Skye again. Just tell him he's great and he'll do whatever you say.' A stupid monkey, is what I am. I don't know what I am, really."

"I won't argue with the monkey part," said Wyatt, a half-smile on his face. "But I didn't know the rest."

"Whoa! Did anybody else hear that?" Shelby stood and put both arms out. We all got quiet and listened, thinking there might be another bear hulking in the forest.

"What?" I whispered.

"Wyatt just apologized!"

"Ha ha," said Wyatt.

"Did he?" I asked. "I didn't hear an apology."

"That's as close as you'll get, is my guess," said Shelby.

"I think it's great," I said to Skye. "Not being 'just the soccer player,' I mean. Now you can be whatever you want."

"That's just it," said Skye. "That's the part I liked. I didn't have to decide. It was decided for me, but it also made things easier. Like, I could go along for the ride knowing I was really good at something, even if I didn't totally love it."

"What do you totally love?" said Wyatt.

"I love to fish."

"Your dad will like that," I said.

"No. He hates that. He wants me to go to college, and with a soccer scholarship I could have afforded it. He never could. He thinks I'm throwing away the future he never had. That's why I was so worried on the drive. But why can't I decide what I want for my own life? So maybe in a few years I'll hate still being in Idaho, but let me figure that out for myself, right?"

"Right," said Shelby. "I feel that way sometimes too. People write me off, though, because they think I fit with girls like Lissy, when I really don't know where I fit. If at all. And my parents never think I'm doing enough."

"You can fit wherever you want to," I said.

"Can I?" asked Shelby. "Would you and your friends let me hang with you? They wouldn't make fun of me?"

"I don't have any friends," I said. "I have a dog. And my grandpa. And lots of dead people." They all looked at me with confused faces. "The cemetery, I mean."

"I get the parental expectations thing," said Wyatt. "My dad always says I don't work hard enough. He tries to exorcise the gay out of me every day, like it's something I should be ashamed of."

Everybody was quiet. Wyatt stared over the fire, small dots reflecting in his eyes. I dodged the smoke so I could see his face.

"What did you just say?" said Shelby.

"Does that make you uncomfortable, Skye?" said Wyatt.

"Not at all," said Skye.

I looked around the fire at the other faces. Skye was leaning closer to the fire, as if trying to catch a smirk from Wyatt, as if Wyatt was out for another laugh and nothing more, as if Wyatt was doing his usual thing.

"This better not be a joke, man," said Skye.

We were all quiet. We'd all heard different rumors over the last couple years at school, but wrote them off immediately because, well, it was *Wyatt*.

"Yes, I'm gay. The rumors are true. I figured you all knew by now."

We were quiet for a beat, staring into the fire.

"So, is that, like, something you can decide to change if you want to?" said Shelby.

Wyatt shrugged, and there was a hint of kindness in his voice when he said, "Why don't you just *decide* to grow your hair out?"

Shelby touched her wig, almost automatically. "Oh," she said quietly. "I get it."

"That's who he is, Shelby," I said. "It isn't something you

can change. And it isn't something you should ever feel you need to change."

"Then why not let people know?" Shelby asked. She stole the toasted marshmallow off Skye's stick just as he pulled it from the fire.

"You know, guys, I want to share something too," said Skye, standing. "I don't know if you know this about me, but . . . well, I'm missing a leg."

Wyatt laughed—loud and genuine—and Shelby and I joined right in.

"Truth is, I wish I could hide this. It changes the way people look at me," said Skye. "So, yeah, I get why you wear a wig, Shelby."

Shelby offered Skye another marshmallow to replace the one she stole. Skye smiled and accepted the peace offering.

"So, why the prepper getup?" I asked Wyatt, unsure if it was too soon to ask something like that or if it was too insensitive.

"I never want to feel like I need to rely on someone else to survive. And it's not, like, a cover for my identity. But can't a person be gay and love art—and also love guns and hunting and horses? The art thing has been approved, right? Society has *allowed* it. But the other stuff? Why not?"

"Sounds like my parents," said Shelby. "I never do enough. I never *am* enough."

We all knew that about Shelby—not that she didn't do enough, but that her parents were never pleased. Gossip rose and fell in our small town like the water below the dam, but the rumors never lasted long. Well, not usually. Some did, like rumors of Nash and that day on the river. Or of Chisum. Or like rumors of Shelby's parents' divorce and all the money they were splitting up and how it had become like a cancer, eating away at any tissue keeping the family together.

Like the rumor that Wyatt's dad beat him on nights when he was real sauced or just pissed, or when he'd head to the Knotty Pine and pick a fight with the biggest Neanderthal in the place. Now we knew he did it because his son was gay and didn't fit with his idea of how the world tilted.

Like rumors of Skye and the way his parents had split years before and how Skye spent most of his time with his dad in the summer, fishing, and only stayed with his mom during the school year, and how they were crazy hard on him about grades and sports and getting out of Idaho and getting a good degree and supporting himself with a job that didn't rely completely on tourism and good weather and the uncertain economics of small towns.

After a long silence, Wyatt spoke up. "I'm working on this post right now about light. I'm thinking of turning it into my essay for college applications. Got the idea from your grandpa, Indie." He muffled the last couple words, his mouth filled with sticky marshmallows. He passed me his stick. "Try one. They're good. Even with the bear spit."

"Grandpa? Is it about a mortuary? Sounds dark." I accepted the stick and moved closer to Wyatt, so I could access the good coals for roasting.

"No. I was trying to corner the paint that had gotten out again, and had the hackamore in my hand, when your grandpa showed up to help. Stepped right out of his trailer and shouted my way, said I was doing it wrong."

"Sounds like Grandpa," I said.

"But he was so kind about it. When we got the horse reined in, we got to talking, and he mentioned his great-grandpa. I can't remember how we got on the subject, but he said his great-grandpa used to work in the Idaho mines. He told me about the Pottok horses the miners used. The horses have these small, sturdy legs for hauling heavy loads and can maneuver in tight spaces. But the craziest part is that the horses would go blind if they were brought to the surface after years of being down below in the mines, in the darkness."

Wyatt stared into the fire, totally lost in the story, not caring to look elsewhere to gage reactions. I was spinning my marshmallow-roasting stick and watching the white mass darken.

"Some horses would have layer upon layer of cloth wrapped tightly over their eyes and around their heads when brought to the surface. Each week, another layer would be removed, slowly letting light in.

"Eventually, they could see again. Imagine it: finally witnessing the surface, the light, the vibrant colors. All those dots of color, like an impressionist painting. And seeing it again, for the first time, a second time. Right? I can't stop thinking about it."

Wyatt's body relaxed, like he'd shifted a weight from himself to the rest of us, and we all felt it and opened our arms and held it up against one another. I thought of responding, but didn't know what to say.

"Sounds like your dad isn't ready to be brought to the surface," said Skye. "He's still got the wraps on, thinking sight can only be about one thing. Not all those colors."

Wyatt smiled. Because he was seated next to me, I could see the wrinkles near his eyes, and I thought I saw his eyes well with tears, but I couldn't be certain in the firelight.

"That's going to be a sweet essay," I said. "Light in art, lightness, darkness, the oil painting of an identity. Letting the light in. Removing the layers."

"All those colors," said Skye, staring straight into the fire.

"It's no big deal," said Wyatt, sheepishly.

"It is a big deal," said Skye, "because it makes you *you,* man." He caught himself. "Sorry. I'm used to saying *man,* but it doesn't change what I said."

"It's all good, Skye," said Wyatt.

Just then, Shelby removed her wig and tossed it in the fire. It lit up with bright sparks and popped loudly for a moment before burning bright and disappearing into the school of scarlet fishes at our feet.

"Yeah she did," said Wyatt.

"I can't witness all this awesome opening up and stay beneath that thing. It itches to high hell, and I'm sick of it."

"No filter," said Wyatt.

"I only said 'hell.' But thanks, Dad," said Shelby.

"No," said Wyatt. "I mean, you always put 'No filter' on your posts, right?"

"You follow me?"

"Who doesn't?" I said.

"You've got tons of stalkers, Shelbs," said Skye. "But at least we're the nice kind."

Wyatt grinned. "I think it would be awesome if you started putting 'No wig,' or 'No fake,' or something like that under

your posts. I bet you'd get way more followers. I'd be more interested in your posts if I knew you were really being you."

Before Shelby could respond, I cut in.

"He's right, Shelby," I said. "You have hundreds of followers,
right?"

"Seven hundred and eighty-six," she said. "As of two days
ago."

"So, you're just ballparking it," said Skye.

"I bet you could get thousands if you put up a video and
owned your baldness. Serious." I pulled the crisp shell of the
marshmallow off the stick and ate it, putting the rest back into
the fire.

"You think so?"

"Being seen as you *truly* are? That's probably the best thing
you can do in this life," said Wyatt.

"Much easier said," said Skye, throwing another rock into
the coals.

"I'm okay with you guys seeing this," said Shelby. "It's such
a relief. But I don't think I can go back to school and let everyone see me like this."

"Because it's really you," said Skye.

"I like the videos because they are once removed, you know?
Not in person. Not like this."

"But you like this, right?" I said, gesturing to all of us sitting
around the fire.

"I love it. But it's not realistic. It's a reality here, but I can't
take this back and set it up at home. It wouldn't work."

"How do you know it won't work? Make it a reality at
home," I said. I set the stick in the fire and let it all burn.

Wyatt nudged me, mock-horrified, and then grabbed another stick and claimed the bag of marshmallows.

"You know," said Wyatt, cutting in, perhaps sensing, as I did, that Shelby was being pushed a little too far and too fast for her liking, "we are all more than one thing, and that's how things should be."

"What do you mean?" said Skye.

"Mrs. Lutz taught us that light is both a particle and a wave, right?"

"Oh, she never stopped talking about that," I said.

"You were listening?" Skye said to Wyatt. "I never thought you were listening in any class. Too cool for class. Too focused on getting back outside to track animals or build something."

"You are good at generalizing, Skye," he said.

"We all are," I said.

"Whatever. If you really want to know, I have a 4.0, and I don't plan on that changing," said Wyatt.

"Yeah, right," said Shelby.

"The fact that nobody believes it is probably a testament to it being true," I said.

"Thanks, Indie."

"So, what about light being two different things?" asked Skye.

"We only see the difference when we observe it closely," said Wyatt. "The world tells us we can't be multiple things, but screw that. Be what you want. Be a particle and a wave. Light bends just like the river, but only when we see it correctly. One path is set until we decide to look, then it all changes. Maybe we are all just finally looking."

"Or seeing," I said. My brain was on fire with this possibility. The night was colored day by this idea, and it was all I could see and taste and feel.

We were all trying to be multiple things, while thinking we could only be one. One thing. But sometimes you have to let things go to survive, right? That was what Nash had said. Let go of it. People matter—not the things. Be the thing that allows you to be you. Don't let people corner you into being just one. Be both.

"This sounds great," said Shelby, "but that's because we're river friends. And this is river life. But I know when we get back to Tetonia and Driggs and real life, things will turn back like they always have. Like they always do. We won't be sitting around a fire and yacking about how great things could be."

"She's right," said Wyatt.

"Doesn't have to be that way," I said.

"Yes, it does," said Shelby. "But at least for another two days I can go without a wig. Pass the marshmallows."

The conversation naturally died out, and Skye pulled out his piece of rope and began practicing climbing knots. Shelby went to her tent to read, and Wyatt said he was going to sketch, leaving me with Skye and the fire and the faint smell of burnt fish, burnt wig, and burnt marshmallows.

I looked over and saw that Nash had a light on, the outline of his squatting body visible through the sheer orange wall of his tent. Maybe he was doing yoga?

"Sorry," I said, without looking at Skye.

"For what?"

"For last night," I said.

"You don't have to apologize."

"I don't have to, but I want to. Maybe you really do want to get to know me. I'm just not used to that. I'm not used to standing next to Shelby and being looked at. It's just something I have to process. And the whole coincidences thing kind of irritated me for some reason."

"Look, if I am right, and we were supposed to be on this river together, then that means I was 'supposed' to lose my leg and any hope of a scholarship or a life I could make sense of, right?" Skye walked around the fire and sat next to me.

"That sounds harsh," I said.

"But even though I don't believe in coincidences, I also don't think we're like some animals and birds, with everything hard-wired into our brains when we're born."

"I don't follow you," I said.

"I hope not. Because then I'd have to call the cops. Another stalker."

"Ha ha. I don't mean it that way. And *another*?"

"You followed me to breakfast this morning, didn't you?"

"No, I mean, mentally."

"You seem a bit mental. It's true," he said.

"Wow. You're the worst, and we're still, like, kind of on the first leg of the journey."

"Really—stooping to a leg joke? I thought you were better than that. But I would like to know, now that you've forgiven me and all, what your position is."

"Shortstop."

"I mean, on us."

"Electrons don't have a definite position. Why should I?" I said.

"Are you going to science your way out of this conversation? You're not an electron."

"So I don't matter?"

"What?" said Skye.

"I am matter, and matter has electrons, so either I don't have a definite position, or I don't matter. You choose," I said.

"Four-letter word for 'confused'?" said Skye.

"Hug," I said.

"What?"

"It's only three letters, but it feels like a bigger word when you act it out."

Before Skye could move, I saw my options in the fire, right in front of us, waiting for me to choose one.

1. *Tell him I have a severely contagious foot fungus that has spread to my entire body, and if he moves closer, he might contract the thing.*
2. *Deflect, now that things are a little more serious. Say something about someone else instead of myself. Never myself.*
3. *Ask him about his past and get him talking.*
4. *Hug and kiss him and scare him with my forwardness and then list all of the NBA power forwards I can think of.*

"There has to be a better word that's actually four letters," said Skye, leaning closer.

"I don't know what it is," I said.

I guess I'd unwittingly chosen option number 4, but I left

off the last part, because I didn't care to talk about NBA players in that moment. I don't know why I said it. Scratch that. I know why I said it. I wasn't ready to say it in that moment. Scratch that. I was totally ready and wanting it and I knew what I was doing and what I wanted him to do and I leaned in just a little and let him go the rest of the way and then he did. He kissed me. And it was wonderful. And it wasn't confusing at all. And it mattered. I knew that. He knew that.

We also knew that tomorrow we'd meet up with Thatcher and Sawyer at camp three, and they'd have supplies and food and new clothing.

What we couldn't know is that we would never make it to camp three, and Nash would be without a satellite phone and in the worst position with any rafting crew that he'd faced in over thirty years of guiding.

What we all wish we knew is just how fast water can change a landscape, and a life.

SEVEN

The sun was a faceless orange coin in the sky. The canyon had its own language. The trees gathered together that next morning and said, *Yes, a light breeze today.* A sweet smell rode on that morning air, on that light breeze, and I hoped it was breakfast. Skye was cooking fish again, and Nash had set out the eggs on a makeshift table near the fire.

I watched Skye tuck the fish into the fire, and I thought of all my fishing back home, of the browns staging on the shallow, rocky corners, prepping for the spawn, of the middle narrows of the Tetons in October, of the float from Riverside down to Hatchery Ford and from the Lower Narrows to Henry's Fork, where I would often let my line float the riffs, the seams in the water, and hook a lunker before tossing it back in to assuage the river gods and what Nash might call karma. I thought of what Grandpa said about letting the fish run, and imagined pulling up on the rod too fast. Like Grandpa says, that's a good way to give the fish a sore lip, but not a good way to land it.

The heat of the morning pressed down upon me as I stepped from the pines and into the sunlight. I saw Shelby taking a video while doing yoga with Nash. It was a completely unexpected thing to see, and I wondered if both of them had let the apple butter slide completely off the biscuit. She had her phone set up on a log, recording their warrior poses. As odd as that was to see, what made me happy was seeing that Shelby wasn't wearing a wig, but had a bandana wrapped around her head instead.

"You going to post that?" I asked as I walked past them.

"I run a fitness gram as well."

"Wish I could double tap your forehead to give you a like right now."

Shelby smiled and changed poses, and Nash followed suit, after nodding a good morning my way. I returned it half-heartedly.

"Where's Wyatt?" I said, making my way to the fire, where Skye was checking on the fish.

"He's over there."

Wyatt was practicing throwing his hatchets into a log that had toppled from atop a boulder beneath a copse of trees that stood like sentinels, watching over the river.

"He was sketching earlier. He's a true Renaissance man," said Skye. "If only we'd known."

"There are a lot of things I want to say that about," I said. "If only I'd known. I want to see what's in that book of his. I want him to tell me more about light in art. That sun is breathtaking. I don't want to get all sentimental, but look at it."

"I'm looking at what's breathtaking," he said, staring my way.

"Funny. I'm looking at the Skye. Too easy."

I heard the slap of small waves against the rocks near the

camp. Skye turned the fish, and I watched the embers wax and wane in the morning light.

"Here's something weird I've been thinking about," said Skye.

It was such an odd transition, I wasn't sure how I was supposed to respond. "Okay?"

"I thought of it while fishing this morning."

"Okay?"

"I don't know. I guess I just think you need to rethink letting it run. That's a phrase people throw around on the river, but I think you understand what I'm getting at."

"Do I?"

"Look, I heard you guys talking when we were placing those stones. You can't just stand next to Nash and hope people see the history and make the decision for you. You've gotta make a move. You can't keep him on the line like that. You can't let him run. You have to release him."

The fishing terminology was something I connected with, and Skye knew it. And I knew I couldn't leave Nash hanging for much longer without making a decision one way or another. Partial forgiveness or hinted-at forgiveness is not forgiveness at all.

"How would that work, then? If you were in my place?"

"I thought you knew how to fly-fish, Indiana. C'mon. Catch and release. All of Idaho would be ashamed to hear you ask that."

"Once again, you're a real sidesplitter this morning. I mean about the forgiveness part, the idea behind it all."

"You ever been to Canada? That's one place I'd like to go fly-fishing."

"You ever stay on topic?" I said.

"Not if I can avoid it."

"Avoid the topic or the staying-on-topic thing as a whole?"

"Canada. I avoid Canada," he said.

"Too much niceness in one place?"

"Too much maple syrup in one place."

"Stereotype much?" I said.

"I'm just wary of my sugar intake. I don't think my pancreas could take it if I moved to Canada."

"Why would you move to Canada?"

"Wow. Non sequitur much? I'm trying to talk about forgiveness, and letting it run, and catch and release."

"I think I'll go throw hatchets with Wyatt instead."

He turned the fish over and checked with his knife to see if the meat was cooked through, the rows of white like snowdrifts in Victor on cold January mornings in the new sun.

"I've just heard life is better when you make peace."

He said it so loudly I turned before making it all the way to Wyatt's spot.

"Show Nash that you're ready to let it go," said Skye. "To show forgiveness. To show it's over."

A few minutes later, Skye leaned back and shouted that breakfast was ready, as he took the fish off the fire.

We all picked at the trout before us. I noted Shelby's continued aversion to fish, and the way Nash only ate the eggs. I ate some of those as well. We had food, just not a lot of options.

"Won't be but a few hours until we have some more food and we can let Skye off the hook."

Nash's attempt at a joke fell flat, though Skye gave him a courtesy laugh. Skye made big eyes at me after and smiled. He sat by me as we finished breakfast.

I thought of the options I had before me concerning the whole letting it run business and forgiveness.

1. *Wait until the last day, and right before hopping into Grandpa's car, shout "I forgive you!" and Nash would never really know who that was meant for or if he could forgive himself.*

2. *Tell Nash how much it hurts not having Mom around. Ask him what he misses about her. Remind him that she cared a great deal about their friendship, and that it was just an accident.*

3. *Bury one of Wyatt's hatchets by the Snake River, after telling Nash it's time to make peace.*

4. *Maintain the status quo, avoid 1 through 3, hurry off the water, and remind myself that I got to know Shelby and Wyatt and Skye on this trip, and that forgiveness wouldn't bring Mom back anyway.*

I landed somewhere between numbers 1 and 3, but I still wasn't sure I could ever really stick to one option. Nash had already prepped the oars, and as we all loaded our gear and stepped into the boat, he gave us another speech about our PFDs and keeping our feet downriver and what it meant when he yelled "High side!"

We were all, like, criminally negligent when it came to

understanding his terminology, as evidenced by Skye and Shelby's spill the day before, so we tried to pay closer attention.

Once we got on the river, I watched as the light reached over the canyon wall and continued on until a strong, orange light brooded over the water.

I noticed, in the distance, a swarm of clouds gathering. From my position, I could only see the heads of the clouds, but they were a full gray with silver linings and large silver bellies, and their massive, pillowy bodies looked as if they were resting on the rim of the canyon.

I heard the morning call of an eagle echoing over the water, and when I listened to the sound bounce back and hover over us, I thought about what it meant to see more than one thing in somebody else. People often find God in church or prayer or religious ceremonies or out in nature, but I seem to find spirituality, or whatever you want to call it, in other people. Like Skye.

The eagle's cry also made me think of when my mother once hit the middle C of our piano and let the sound bounce around the room before saying, "Node."

At first, I thought she'd said "Note," and I didn't know how to respond, but she explained that a node in a room is all about proper resonances of sound. Certain sounds in certain rooms fit perfectly together. Throw in a key, get a symphony back in return. I couldn't help but wonder that morning if I was throwing out a key and letting it echo off the canyon walls only to get back a symphony from Skye sitting next to me. From the entire group, really. It's like we'd spread out the weight of a lifetime of secrets we'd been hoarding, and we could now carry the load together, even if it meant carrying it on a death-noodle down a raging river.

"First up, we got Waterspout Rapids, team," said Nash, his arms turning at odd angles as he sloped the raft past an eddy and into the faster-moving current, his arms like stork legs in motion. "They'll wake you up, if the sun hasn't already."

"I want a pastry to wake me up. Not the sun," I said.

"I want a cronut," said Shelby.

"That sounds amazing," said Wyatt.

"Maple syrup going to be at camp three?" said Skye.

"Or an ice-cream cone," said Shelby.

"I'm not trying to be mean, Shelbs," said Wyatt, "but can't you have your mom or dad, like, Uber Eats in some pizza or something on a helicopter?"

"Right. I'll just have them see which helicopters are in the area and on shift."

"Thanks," said Wyatt.

They'd completely derailed Nash's instructions, but I was happy for the conversation. I felt like all my problems had found a new place to hide in the three sitting next to me. But that also made me worry that my problems would come rushing back the second we separated. We only had two days left on the water. For that, I was happy, because it meant only a few days left with Nash. But when I looked at the soft faces in the morning light and the way they all smiled at one another and the way we'd kind of become friends, it made me sad.

"We'll have everything we need at the next camp," said Nash. "Even pastries."

A tongue of water sat fifty yards away, pulling surrounding

water in briskly. The rapids loomed larger than any set we'd seen on the river so far. I was worried there was a waterfall on the other side of the two boulders staring my way, because of the noise echoing in the background. Where the currents meet in the river, it turns to color and sound and not much else above the roar of the water. Rhythm and bounce; shimmy and spray.

"Hold onto yourselves. This water is going to spray hard, and it won't quit until we run this line. Some rocks will have pillows because of the way the water is collected, so be prepared to start and stop with each move. At the end, we'll hit a massive hydraulic. This one is going to be really technical. I'm going to peel out of this eddy here when you all give me the go-ahead. I can't go into this one without a thumbs-up from every one of you."

Sometimes Nash said things like questions, as if he was unsure of the right line to take and was looking for the go-ahead from me in particular. He always looked my way, like maybe I could see the line better. That may have been true, considering I spent so much time on the Snake River.

Nash put his ponytail in a bun beneath his hat, which seemed odd, considering how wet we were going to get. Maybe it was some kind of nervous tic. Skye looked ready, but then Skye was the type of guy who could decide to do an ultra-marathon without training a day in his life and still get, like, a really respectable time. But none of the rest of us were exceptionally athletic or overly attractive or anything. Okay, maybe Shelby and Wyatt were. I watched as Shelby readied herself, sitting up straighter, the bandana around her head catching dappled light. She was so pretty in that moment, even sans hair.

It was odd to be friends with someone like Shelby. She was so popular, and the way she looked, the way she commanded attention with her bright eyes, suggested she could leave us all behind in a moment and hop into another life without a second thought and be even more successful, even happier, even prettier. I wished I had that kind of poise.

I looked back at Nash as I gave my thumbs-up and saw some small emotion—annoyance or uncertainty or fear—flicker across his sunbaked, wrinkled face like a passing breeze, and then it was gone. There was some odd apprehension in the way he used his control hand to turn the oar and guide us to the rapids up ahead. And then he was peeling out from the eddy and leading the raft to the tongue, and I couldn't do anything to stop what happened next.

What happened next: We dipped into the water sluicing between the boulders at the start of the rapids. The haystack waves were massive. They were so big that when we decelerated against the built-up upstream water, a standing wave was waiting for us when the raft dipped back into the faster waters.

We were soaked after pivoting around the first two boulders. The death-noodle was riding high on swells that seemed much larger than any we had previously encountered. Skye was whooping and hollering and screaming into the water as it crashed over us. Shelby had a huge smile, and even Wyatt was laughing. I was in the back and Nash was facing forward, so I couldn't see his expression, but I heard him yell a couple of times.

Streaking rays of light blinded me at one point as I opened my eyes only to find the sun glaring off another swell about to wash over me. The raft decelerated as I shifted my body weight to anticipate the next dip, but I was off by a half-second, and the water knocked me off the raft and into the frothing white of the river.

"Grab a loop!" Nash shouted.

He turned to look at me, but the moment he looked away from the line, the raft wrapped around a boulder and then bounced backwards and dropped into a hole, only to rise immediately after at such a steep gradient that everyone toppled out, including Nash. I saw the bodies flail, and the oar missed me by inches as the water pulled me back under.

I was swallowing far too much water. I rose, and my throat stung as I sucked in air before dropping into another hole, knocking my knee against a boulder. I was aware enough to keep my feet downstream, but I didn't know exactly where I was located on the river; I didn't know which way to swim to avoid a strainer.

Two giant boulders were piled atop one another like unwieldy pancakes, and before I got sucked down once more, I saw ribbons of water snaking through small holes left by the gaps between the rocks. I kicked hard to avoid the narrowing window, but I couldn't escape the pull. I thought of what Nash had said and tried to scrape my way to the surface and go over the strainer, but the pull was beyond my strength. My body was sucked into a hole the size of a doggy door, and I couldn't wiggle free. My head was facing upriver, and I felt the pull of the downstream current on my feet on the other side of the strainer.

I knew I couldn't hold my breath for much longer. My heart was pounding arrhythmically. My lungs felt like they might burst, like they were one of those homemade rockets where you hook the bottle up to a pipe and stomp on it and it shoots the thing into the air. I was drenched in adrenaline, even without the water pulling me in different directions and crushing my air source. Seconds masqueraded as hours.

Pure survival instinct kicked in. Perhaps that's how my arms moved without receiving any signal from my brain, because my brain was shouting "Air!" and my heart felt like it was being pressed up against my chest by a semitruck. I wasn't thinking about unclipping from my PFD, but that's exactly what I did.

After researching what happened to Mom, I knew enough about strainers to know that going through is the only option. Nobody is strong enough to swim against the current pressing with so much force, so many pounds per square inch. Nothing short of an actual rocket could escape such brutal, unforgiving force.

With my PFD unclipped, I slid closer to the boulder and kicked my feet and knew that my last option was to release the rest of the air before I blacked out. I had to be as thin as possible in order to escape the tight window between the two boulders. Between a hard place and a hard place. A rock and a rock. So that's exactly what I did.

All air out, all pull, all ferocity and instinct and gut-panic to survive. I yanked one arm through and felt the granite threaten to turn my arm into chum, but I kept going. I used that arm to pull and kept my other arm straight out in front of my face and wiggled out of my PFD. My entire body made it through the small opening in the strainer just in time for the no-air thing to take control, and I swallowed water as my body shot to the surface with the speed and pressure and wonderful force of the undercurrent of a rapid swell.

I emerged from the water sucking air and coughing simultaneously, and I saw the oar ten yards in front of me. Blood bloomed in the water next to my arm. I saw Wyatt pop up from the water as well, the expression on his face like an exclamation point of activated energy and panic and survival-instinct mode.

I turned my feet downstream and tried to get as much air as I could before I went under again. I attempted to spot any strainers or large limbs or boulders, but before I could reach a high-point to navigate, my foot hyperextended against a log and turned my body sideways, and my head connected with a boulder.

Everything went black.

EIGHT

When I woke, a good amount of blood had gathered and pulsed at the back of my head, and my body was still dripping water. I heard the rapids spray and roil and crash in the background. My side was raw and numb, and my right arm felt like it had been put through a potato slicer. A step away from death. That's how close I'd been.

I turned from my side onto my back and felt an ease wash through me, momentarily, as I recognized the familiar weight of my mother's ring on my chest.

Shelby was sitting next to me, soaked, her features shimmering in the afternoon light. A line of water slid down her bald scalp; I noticed she had a cut on her head and her bandana was gone. She shook her head back and forth like I do at home when I'm trying to get a TV remote to work, hoping it's not the batteries. Her eyes slowly seemed to focus, and she saw me and gave a half-smile and then sat up straighter.

I breathed in through my nose and out through my mouth, trying to release some of the tension in my muscles, in my chest. My arms felt like they'd never been used, like they were unsure of how to press against the ground and lift me up into a sitting position. Every muscle in my body felt weak, like I'd been flexing everything for an entire day only to finally release into relaxation. But the day was only half-over, and I knew I'd need more energy.

Nobody asked about the raft or the gear because everything else seemed unimportant considering what had just happened. I heard Nash screaming twenty yards downriver and saw Wyatt ripping his shirt and wrapping it around Nash's leg. I tried to stand up, but stars burst in my peripheral, and I knew I'd moved too quickly. I sat back down and held my face between my knees and breathed in deeply.

After a minute, I tried again, gathering what strength I had and standing slowly. I saw Skye walk back to Wyatt with a pile of wood. Good. Everyone had made it. As I walked over to them with Shelby, I caught sight of the raft, the black streak set against the lighter blue. It was beached on a tipped grand fir that looked like it had been in the river since time began. The raft wasn't moving.

The waters were slow at this oxbow, and the river looked almost peaceful as it bumped up against the fir with each shift in the water. The raft could come later, though. Shelby put her arm around my shoulders as we joined Nash, Skye, and Wyatt.

"I seriously thought I was going to die," she said.

"Me too," I said. "Are you hurt?"

"Just a few scratches. You?"

"My knee feels a little wonky, but just scratches, otherwise."

The mood around Nash was one of quiet desperation. Wyatt's face told the story—brows fixed and lips pinched and his eyes more serious than I'd ever seen them. Skye stood next to Wyatt, waiting to be told what to do. I looked down at Nash's leg and had to hold back from retching in front of him. I could see bone beneath the wet shirt Wyatt had wrapped around the leg.

"I can't do this," said Shelby, walking back to our previous spot on the shore and sitting. She was the only one still wearing her PFD.

"That will hold for now," said Wyatt. "If anyone sees the red first aid kit, let me know. We could use it."

"It's in the raft," said Nash. "Under my seat."

"We all fell out of the raft," said Skye.

"It's upstream," I said. "Right there."

Wyatt nodded, as if he was in a hospital and this information was news he could work with, though he wasn't about to give the patient any hope just yet.

"Well, the leg is obvious," said Wyatt. "Broken tibia in multiple places, is my guess. I also think that arm is a noodle that needs setting fast. Sorry, Nash. I mean, it will heal, but you won't be walking or rowing for a while."

"I didn't feel the leg as much as the arm," said Nash. He winced in pain and slowly breathed out, holding most of it in his chest like a slow rumble, a soft growl. He was working hard to mask the pain. "My arm caught between two rocks and my body went with the water, twisting as it went, until it popped free as I rose with a swell."

"Spiral fracture, maybe," said Wyatt.

"You an EMT or something?" I said.

"Something like that," said Wyatt.

He didn't look like he wanted to talk about it, and he continued working on Nash's leg until he felt it was sturdy enough to leave it alone. He gently maneuvered Nash's arm into a sling made from torn clothing.

"Don't move that leg. Or that arm. You sit right here," said Wyatt.

He and Skye leaned Nash against a boulder at an angle that looked semi-comfortable, all things considered.

The raft was still upstream, still stuck against a giant log. Nobody knew what gear we had available to us, and we were all soaked in water as well as adrenaline. I was shaking, but wasn't sure if it was my body warming up, or my body trying to contain the adrenaline shooting out from my fingertips.

"We have to see what's in that raft," said Wyatt. "Grab the first aid kit. I need to put something on that leg wound that will hold better than my shirt."

I tried not to stare at Wyatt—considering our situation—but, holy buckets, he was ripped. I knew he had some definition in his arms because we wore PFDs and he sometimes wore smaller shirts, but so often in camp he wore his really baggy zombie apocalypse prepper shirt, and nobody could tell just how toned he was.

Skye looked between us, and then he pulled me aside as Wyatt put his PFD back on and made his way back upstream, heading for the raft.

"You seeing what I'm seeing?" said Skye.

"The raft?"

"That walking god right there. Adonis, I think, is his name."

"Shut up," I said.

"Dang, Indie," said Skye. "Look at your arm."

He was right. I hadn't had time to really look at it, but now I felt its pulsing revive as I stared into what looked like the aftermath of a meat grinder. Luckily, it was all on the surface. No fractures. At least, none that I could feel.

Wyatt waded into the water and slowly made his way toward the raft. The rest of us watched, and I worried that, though the water was slow, something else was about to happen. Perhaps thinking the same thing, Skye ran back to Nash, where he had an oar—the same oar he'd used to help Nash onto shore, I later learned—and walked out to meet Wyatt. Ribbons of gritty sand shifted beneath my feet while I waited.

When Wyatt was next to the raft, he grabbed the guide rope and pulled it free of the log. Thankfully, he was able to find enough purchase to yank the raft back and swim it to shore with the help of Skye and the oar. Shelby and I helped pull the raft onto dry land. We probably pulled it too far, but we were all anxious and worried and novices when it came to beaching-rafts-after-massive-spills-and-serious-injuries kinds of things.

Wyatt emerged from the raft with the first aid kit and ran to Nash. Skye hopped into the raft and began searching through what was left.

"Any food?" I asked.

"No food. Or water, other than two bottles."

"Coke?"

"No Coke, either," said Skye. "But that *would* be more important than food or water or dry clothes, right? All that's left are two tents and our climbing gear, of all things."

"Truly," I said. "Of all things. No fly-rod?"

"My rod is gone. And all the flies," he said.

"Still plenty of flies," I said, swatting at one resting on my shoulder.

"Wrong kind."

"Right kind, wrong make."

"Right," he said, jumping down from the raft with the climbing gear and one of the tents.

We walked back to the others, and Wyatt immediately started setting up the tent, saying we needed to let Nash rest and regroup before we figured out what to do next. Skye filled everyone in on what we had. Or, more accurately, what we *didn't* have.

"Any phones?" Wyatt asked.

Skye shook his head. "Dry-bags are gone. We might see some on our way down the river. Maybe some were caught against the shore somewhere."

"I guess Wyatt won't have a shirt for a while," I said, looking at Shelby for a smile or confirmation. But Shelby's head was between her knees, and I heard her sniff. She was crying. My timing was awful.

"What's wrong?"

"Are you kidding me?" she said, lifting her head. "Look at this. Look at us! How are we supposed to get out of here? I don't recall any of you being able to raft a river like this. Maybe Wyatt can get us out because he's ready for everything. I don't know."

"C'mon, Shelby. That's not fair," I said.

"She's not wrong, though," said Skye. "I'm lucky my leg wasn't lost in that spill. We don't have any way of communicating, do we? I haven't seen another outfit since my groover visit yesterday."

"Wait, you saw another raft while you were at the groover?" I said.

"It was really awkward. I just waved. What was I supposed to do? Ten people just watching me from two different rafts. But at least it was scenic. For all of us."

"Not funny," said Shelby. "Stop joking. Stop flirting, Skye. We ate the last of the food this morning. We have some water left, and what? Cheese?"

"Easy, Shelbs," said Wyatt.

"Don't call me that!"

She stood up and walked beyond the chokecherry shrubs near the water's edge, then climbed over a turned log split halfway up and moldering on the ground.

"She needs to relax," said Skye.

"She's the only one showing the proper amount of fear," said Wyatt. "Look, I hate to say this, but you guys need to understand we're not in a great spot."

"We get that," said Skye, looking my way.

"We can't just hop back into the raft and find help. We have rapids between us and any help, and we can't run them with any certainty that Nash will make it through," Wyatt said.

I screwed my lips up and watched Wyatt finish putting up the tent, the poles connecting and swinging like he was some madman conductor with too-long batons all over the place.

I glanced at Nash, leaning on the nearby boulder. I wondered what it would take for him to get back into the raft.

"Never seen water do that," said Nash, wincing, pulling

his arm closer to his chest, perhaps thinking that would relieve some of the pain.

I gave Nash one of my more withering looks.

"Okay. Maybe one other time," he said.

I had a preternatural feeling in my gut, like everything was out of sync, and yet we were exactly where we needed to be to regroup.

"The next two sets of rapids before Sheep Creek Cabin are supposed to be easier. After that, though . . ." He shook his head. "Indie knows how to find a line in the water. We can't wait here and hope another outfit will find us. We don't have food or water—and I don't think I have that kind of time."

"You must be out of your mind if you think we're getting back on the water with you in your condition," said Skye.

I was thinking the same thing, so I was happy he said it.

"I agree with Shelby. We're screwed," said Wyatt.

"Aren't you the prepper guy," said Skye, "afraid of nothing and nobody?"

"Nice. Another quick judgment, bud," he said. "I'm not without worries over here. Did you see Nash's leg?"

"I don't see any other options here," said Nash. "My crew knows that if we don't make it to camp three, we need help. But I doubt we can make camp three by nightfall. They will look for us, starting with Sheep Creek Cabin, which is our rescue point, if needed. We'll be lucky to make it to the cabin. No radio. No sat phone. No other way of letting them know we're in trouble. They'll be searching for days." He put his hand on his leg, closed his eyes, and tilted his head to the sky.

A bald eagle hovered high above our position, and I

imagined what I'd see in that moment if I were a bird flying high above the canyon walls. I closed my eyes as well, listening to the small breeze brush off the fir trees and pines and whisper through the canyon with the rapid's roar a hush in the background on this side of the oxbow.

Four-letter word for "incorrigible": *Nash*. Someone beyond correcting or improving or changing. I figured he'd brushed over the bit about the sat phone without recognizing what he'd said, because he didn't seem to change his trajectory.

Skye looked at me and knew that I'd caught it—how could I not?

Options:

1. *Grab the oar next to the raft, slowly bring it into a quiet backswing, and then completely KO Nash and let him slump against the rock.*
2. *Scream until my voice gives out completely.*
3. *Ask Wyatt if any of his hatchets made it through the spill, tell Nash I was trained in open-leg surgery, and commence procedure with hatchet.*
4. *Calmly ask why this important information was kept from me.*

I guess I took a spin on numbers 2 and 4, but the entire time I was thinking about 1 and 3.

I looked at Wyatt and Skye. "Did you know about this?"

"About what?" said Shelby, walking back from behind the shrubs, her eyes red and swollen.

"The satellite phone."

"All outfits have a sat phone," said Wyatt. "Where is yours, Nash?"

Nash winced again, but I wasn't sure if it was real or if he was using it to deflect.

"Where is the sat phone, Nash?" I said.

Nash breathed out heavily and cradled his arm.

"I didn't bring one. A luxury I couldn't afford. Look, my guys are close. We can make this. There are always other outfits on the river. I'm the one injured anyway, so don't worry."

"Don't *worry*? Really?" said Wyatt. "We thought you had a sat phone from day one. Isn't it required?"

"Yes, technically," said Nash.

"Technically," repeated Wyatt, staring at Nash. "Nice. That's good. That's great."

"It was a guaranteed connection in case we had something like this happen," said Skye.

"You didn't think to be prepared for an emergency?" I said. "So what was that whole rock pile about, anyway? You didn't learn a thing."

I walked to the raft, grabbed the other tent, and went back around the oxbow, where the shout of the rapids was louder, where the water could work its way into my thoughts and crowd out the betrayal I felt, where the trees would provide me company rather than some group of random strangers and a guide who couldn't be trusted.

No crossword puzzles. No fly-rod. No hatchets. No Bury. No book to read, nobody to talk to, and nowhere to go. Hell on earth. Hell's canyon, on earth, because where else would it be?

Was I being immature? Was I being too hard on Nash, still,

despite all of our efforts to close the gap he created when he hesitated and my mom drowned because of it? Would he have died in the same manner?

What if I'd agreed to go on the river trip with her? What if I'd pulled her back, or made us late so we didn't hit the rapids at the same time, in the same way, and lose anybody to the water? The past circled me like a whirlpool, and I felt the years of anguish billow around me like the silt from a darting fish in the bottom of the river.

My arm was pulsing, the adrenaline slowly ebbing, my body achy and tired and my eyes heavy. The sun was hitting the yellow rain-fly, and I tasted salt and felt rage curl in my stomach.

I knew we had to get back on the water eventually, but I couldn't go out there feeling the way I was feeling. I was sweating in that stupid tent with the yellow rain-fly, and the only reason I had the fly on was to keep anybody from staring at me. I wanted privacy, and it provided what little I could find.

"Anybody in there?"

"Not now, Skye," I said.

"It's me. Wyatt. And I have my shirt off."

"Not gonna work, Skye."

"Worth a shot, though, right?"

"I wanted off this infernal river the first day. I asked about the phone the *first day*. That man is a liar."

"If you hadn't come, it would mean you wouldn't know me. Or Shelby. Or Wyatt. And yes, his lie was stupid, but he didn't want to give you another reason to back out. How could he know something like this would happen?"

"That's just it. It's happened before. Worse. He should plan for it."

"Ultimately, the man lied to find forgiveness. To make peace. He just didn't want you to bail on the trip. He wanted to make things right."

I saw his shadow squat in the sand outside the rain-fly.

"I'd lie for that as well."

I heard him breathe in deeply and out through his nose. He waited. I waited. It was a long silence, and I looked at the tent walls as if they held some sort of answer. The heat was brutal, and I was dripping sweat. My arm ached. Flies buzzed against the tent flaps, nicking against the material.

"I think you should come out so we can spend more time together. I mean, what will you do without me, Indie? If I'm not around after this trip? My guess is that you'll probably wake up one day and start smoking just to keep the pain away, to keep away the thoughts of what we could have been. After a while, you'll realize smoking was a poor decision because everyone at school will only remember you because of your smell, instead of your wonderful personality.

"But by then, you'll be up to a hundred-dollar-a-week habit, and you'll be in debt to some serious bookies, who'll threaten to hurt children if they don't get paid on time. You'll decide to go on the patch to save the children, but those cost a lot as well. You'll realize the only way to get off cigarettes is to go with cheap chewing tobacco, because you can't quit cold turkey, because that just means your mind will race with thoughts of me.

"So you'll fill cups of spit in school, and people will be glad you don't smell, but they'll be grossed out by the red Solo cup you have to carry with you everywhere. Then, you'll lose all your teeth, get a rare flesh-eating disease from the cheap fiberglass in the chew, and need half of your face removed.

"Your dog will try to attack you, and your grandfather will kick you out of the trailer because he doesn't recognize Half-Face—which will be your new nickname at school, obviously—and you'll end up sleeping in one of those ATM booths that you can only access with a bank card, so you'll wait until people need cash, then sneak in behind them and sleep in there.

"Then, because I have a great job during the school year, I'll be the one delivering you pizzas in that ATM booth and asking if you'll reconsider what we could have had if only you'd exited the tent instead of sitting in your anger. At that point, though, you won't be able to get the other half of your face back. And I don't want that. I want to deliver you pizzas, but only if you have a whole face to eat them."

I was glad he couldn't see me smiling. I didn't want to be smiling. I wanted to feel every emotion but joy, and I was working hard to suppress any happiness. Something about the Skye outside the tent.

"Is this your ham-fisted attempt at an apology for Nash? He should do his own apologizing."

"C'mon, Indie. He's had it pretty rough as it is. We were all a step away from death."

"A stroke away from death," I said. "We were swimming. Or trying to. And we would have hit that rapid either way."

"A stroke away from death. Sounds like a diagnosis for someone way too into smoking."

"He lied about that phone. By not being prepared, he put us

in this situation. Like my mom's accident taught him nothing," I said.

"You're right. He keeps writing the same tale. But it's in your hands now. You have the power to change the story."

"It's already written. She's in the ground. Nash is above it. I'm here."

I imagined Skye staring out into the improbable terrain that had almost swallowed us whole, rows of white clouds frozen in the sky like the insides of a trout.

"Leslie Marmon Silko once said that stories never really end."

I heard him move closer to the tent. I could see the outline of his body as he bent over, looking at the rocks by his feet.

"And she doesn't distinguish between history or fiction, fact or rumor. Stories bring people together, keep people together. Words are never alone. They are always encompassed by other words. Words have neighbors, always. Think about your crosswords, Indie. Think about your neighbors. Not the horses. Get it? *Neigh*bors."

"You're worse than my grandpa."

"Worth a shot."

I did think about the crosswords, though. I'd lost those to the water as well. Listening to Skye detail the ways words moved in and out of lives, I realized I'd been quite parsimonious with my ideas of what the future could be without Mom. The water outside rolled over his words. The water was words.

"Stories aren't some line we follow—A to B to C," he said. "Life isn't like that. It's more like a web, Indie. It forms as it is told, and you get to decide what it means. You get to decide how to change the story."

"A story of being stuck," I said.

"Nobody knows rivers like you do. You don't have to forgive him right now, but we need you on that river."

I was silent. I didn't know how to respond. I grabbed the necklace at my throat. I wondered in that moment if what had seemed accidental was actually essential. Like, some cosmic joke on me: Nash had to be the guide because I had to figure out how to forgive. But that sounded too easy and had nothing to do with my abilities on the water.

But at least it was an idea I could keep separate from the fact that I was thirsty and hungry and injured, just like the rest of our group, and I was being stubborn and staying in the tent instead of moving forward to safety or hope or whatever there was to be had from our situation.

"You know," Skye said, "when people go mountain climbing, they have to be careful to avoid crevasses."

"You just like saying that word."

"Maybe."

I was silent again.

"There are crevasses that are more than a hundred and fifty feet deep. If you fall, you're a goner."

"This is very uplifting," I said.

Skye ignored my comment. "If you fall into a crevasse and survive, what are your options?"

"You have to climb out," I said. "Obviously."

"True. But with some crevasses, if you follow them down as far as you can, they can lead to another opening at a different spot on the mountain. Going down into the darkness can some-times lead to the only light you're going to find."

"So you're saying I need to think darker thoughts and swim to the river bottom?"

"I'm saying you need to go through this. Not over it, not under, not around. And it might also be true that you need to go deeper with Nash, and maybe then you'll find an out. You keep thinking you can avoid it, but you're already in the cre-vasse. Maybe it's time you rappel down into the darkness."

I listened to him breathe outside the tent and shift his weight. I put my head between my knees and tried to clear my mind. The only thing I kept thinking of was that line Mom al-ways said: "Knowledge. Everything and everyone deserves to be sought after and known." I stepped from the tent a few minutes later and helped Skye stand up.

"You ready to forgive?"

"I don't know. But I do know we need to get moving if we are going to make it to that stupid cabin and help the moron who put us in this situation without any way to call for help."

"Mercy is only mercy when it's given to the people we don't want to have it, who we don't think are deserving of such a thing."

Skye was working his way into my life, and I didn't know if I'd ever be the same. I felt like I had giant canyons forming in my chest. With enough time, a river can carve through any-thing. With enough time, so can a person.

NINE

Curious. I watched the clouds in the distance slide slowly our way on their silvery bellies. It was late in the afternoon, and the tents were packed and the raft was functional and our plan was to continue on to the Sheep Creek Cabin and wait for help. I think we were all hoping that there might already be some help there from other outfits.

Nash said that there were numerous cabins in the area owned by other crews and that we were bound to find help. Surprisingly, aside from the outfits Skye had seen, we'd seen no one on the water for almost two days. No satellite phone, no radio, no cell phones, and no other way out. We had the climbing gear and two water bottles and two tents. And each other.

Nash was asleep, and Wyatt said that the longer he slept, the better. We managed to carry him to the raft without waking him and even secured him using the climbing gear. Wyatt said the trauma to Nash's body was enough to knock most people out, which is why our jostling hadn't woken him.

We were all breathing heavily by the time we got Nash in the raft, our feet squeaking against the urethane.

"When a person dies, their sense of hearing is the last thing to go," I said.

"I'll take 'Weirdest Thing Ever Said' for $200, Alex," said Skye.

"It's true. Grandpa told me that one day when I was helping him at the mortuary."

"So cool," said Wyatt.

"Can we just get moving?" Shelby said.

"I can still hear you, Shelbs. Good news—I'm not dead," said Wyatt.

I could tell she was tense, and not excited to talk about, well, anything. She held one of the water bottles, and Wyatt told her to take it easy. She passed it around so we could all have a sip.

Wyatt told us the human body could go for more than three weeks without food, but only a week without water—and only a few days if we wanted to stay sharp mentally. With the heat, Wyatt gave us two days without water before we'd be in serious trouble.

Shelby looked at the nearly empty water bottle in her hand, then at us.

I watched the river and thought of the trout in the cool pockets beneath the water. I imagined sending out a fly-line with Hoppers and Chernobyl Ants on the end and snagging something beautiful. Catch and release. We'd almost lost Nash that afternoon, released into the water like Mom. All of us had, in fact.

Curiously, what little heat weighed down the air was washed away almost immediately on a breeze that rushed through the canyon like a destroying angel. Those large, silver clouds hovered over the canyon walls, and then their silver bellies turned to black and that blackness gathered weight and that weight gathered sound and that sound rumbled in our chests when the first boom echoed out over the water. A storm was upon us.

I pushed us into the slow waters and stood in the middle of the boat. I was afraid to sit and get comfortable for even a moment, knowing two sets of rapids stood between us and safety and rescue.

We watched the sun dip behind the canyon wall and felt a collective shiver run through us, knowing that we might be facing more water. This time from above.

"Maybe we should have kept the tents set up and waited? Surely someone would find us," said Shelby.

"Can't take that chance," said Wyatt. "Nash is too banged up."

Water from above, water from below, and not a drop to drink. Earlier, I'd considered it a race against the sun, but without the sun, I wasn't sure how far we could make it. I knew we'd have to move quickly.

Rain began to fall in earnest as we approached the first set of rapids. Nash started to shift in his slouched, roped-in position, the rain pelting his face. Were he awake, he could tell us what the rapids were called. I called them a hellish nuisance, but he might have had a more precise term for them.

I tried to forget about the wreck, about my arm that Wyatt had bandaged up after tending to Nash, about the water pouring down on top of us, and I focused on the line.

I watched as the water split in several places at once, all

circling the same boulder garden we were about to fall into. The water gathered and slipped away, like a logic that defied understanding, like chaos. I recognized the green in the water directly before us, a dark fan of shadow below the first lip of water, the storm already shifting the colors of the river.

"Hold on tight. We can't afford another spill," I said, almost shouting because of the thunderstorm on top of us. I eased us into the first tongue of water.

The raft rose with the white-tipped waves and crashed, water spraying our faces. I imagine it's what buckshot would feel like from a distance, those hard pellets of water.

I braced against the features with a paddle and felt my arm start to give, the mounting pressure pushing back. I was on high alert and was not about to let more carnage happen. At one point, Shelby slipped as we got caught between two merging swells, but Wyatt grabbed her PFD and pulled her back into the raft.

The line I picked was relatively calm, but the water was rising with the storm, and I was losing sight of the currents and their distinct patterns in the river.

It was a bony section of water, but the line kept us straight and true until we shot out into relatively calm waters on the other end. Calm, but still moving at a good clip. It looked like it was raining upward, the water hitting the river and the river rising to meet it. We rose over a small boil before descending again into a softer flow. But the rain was so heavy I couldn't see my line anymore.

Nash woke coughing, and wiped the water from his eyes. "Are we out yet?"

"We're out of that set, but I can't see any lines anymore," I said.

"We need to run the Rush Creek Rapids to get to the cabin," said Nash.

"Did you not hear me?" I shouted. "I can't see anything."

I wasn't about to argue with the man half-out of his mind with pain as we neared the next set of rapids without any visual. The water was churning and shooting up in spikes, and I wasn't going to put our lives in another set of rapids without a sight line. I'd been on this river before, but not like this.

I used the paddle to control the raft, sending us into a shore-line eddy and up onto the rocky beach. There were not a lot of trees for shelter, at least not many I could see close by, but I thought there was a small copse twenty yards from the raft. The rate of rainfall on my face made it hard to decipher much with any amount of clarity.

"This is outrageous," said Shelby. "I can't see anything."

I wiped at my eyes as everyone quickly hopped out of the raft. Wyatt grabbed one tent, and Skye grabbed the other.

We retreated to the nearest pine trees. Wyatt dropped the tent and ran back to help me untie Nash. Standing in the raft, I realized the water had already risen to my ankles. I wondered if we had not pulled in far enough, or if the storm had merely increased in intensity. I had a hard time keeping my footing while helping Nash out of the raft. Shelby hurried to my side and helped with Nash as we waddled awkwardly to the trees.

Wyatt immediately set up the tent poles, and we hurried to create our shelter. Skye was attempting to set up one of the rain-flies over the ground next to the trees. The trees provided enough protection from the storm that we could see what we were doing. Wyatt dragged the bottom tarps closer to a large tree with a small ring of dry ground near the base, and we were able to set up one tent in minutes. We all helped Nash into the tent and zipped it up.

"Hang the fly on that branch," Wyatt said. "It's too muddy. I'm not going to worry about stakes. Help Skye. If we can get enough space, we can start a fire."

Lightning flashed in the distance. It beaded and forked in the sky, and I saw it shoot one solitary bolt straight into the canyon, miles beyond our position. A field south of us was pooling water in small pockets in the sagebrush and bunchgrass. We stood near the front door of the tent, dripping.

"What are we going to do?" I said.

"Die, probably," said Shelby.

"C'mon, Shelby, we'll be okay. It's just a little rain," said Skye.

"We have to secure the raft with the climbing rope first," said Wyatt. "I can use the guide rope as well, with the carabiners on there. While I'm doing that, I need you guys to take whatever can hold water and place it at the sloped end of this tent-fly. We can collect drinking water. Skye, get to work on a fire."

"With what?"

"I usually start with wood," said Wyatt.

"Ha," said Skye. "No dry wood. No flint. No lighter."

"Crap," said Wyatt, grumbling as he ran from the trees to check on the raft.

I was so happy Wyatt was there. I wanted to hug him when he returned from securing the raft, and then realized that without his shirt on it might seem a little, well, much. Plus, he had his PFD on, so hugging him would be like trying to keep a massive ball between us and not letting it drop or get in the way of our faces. Hint: impossible.

Skye stood in the opening of the trees and let water fall on his head and roll down his face before watching it drop to the ground or trail down his limbs. He stared at his leg, and then lowered his head.

I walked to him and grabbed his hand and led him back to the tent. "We have no fire. We need to get dry and stay dry," I said.

He sat in the tent and removed his PFD and his shirt, and I had to admit he was giving Wyatt a run for the Adonis title. Skye sat next to Nash, who had again passed out.

Shelby ducked down into the tent and took off her PFD and shirt, leaving her with her bikini top and board shorts. I did the same.

Wyatt joined us and checked on Nash. He helped him remove his shirt—more by ripping it off than taking it off because of his arm—and get as dry as possible.

"We need to get warm," he said, ditching his PFD. "I gave Nash most of the pain meds, so I hope he'll be feeling better soon. At least for a bit. We can't stay like this for long, though. We need to warm each other up. Hypothermia can set in pretty fast."

Shelby looked at me. I stared back at her, then at Skye.

"You know if our body temperature falls below 95, we're done for," said Wyatt. "We'll go from shivering to reduced circulation to slow-breathing, followed by irritability, lack of coordination, sleepy behavior, confusion, and a weak pulse. Let's not let it get past stage one."

"That's why we're in here," said Skye.

"Stay close. Stay warm," said Wyatt.

"Right," said Shelby, scooting closer to me.

"Actually, guys, it'd be better if you spoon and share body heat that way. I know it sounds super awkward or whatever, but it'll help you stop shivering. We're not going to get warmer without any dry clothes or a fire."

We looked at one another. Paused.

"C'mon, guys. It's how birds stay alive when it's cold. Just do it," said Wyatt.

The water was still dripping onto the mesh above us, as our fly was being used to cover what we had hoped would have been a firepit. With that option out, we didn't move the fly and were left with more water getting in. I stepped out and quickly adjusted the fly to allow for some cover from the raindrops coming from the pine needles above, and I saw Wyatt kneeling near the door. I could barely see out to the river at that point.

Shelby was spooning Skye, shivering, her lips a darker color than they'd been earlier and her eyes sunken into her wet face, and said, "It's not what it looks like, Indie."

"It's exactly what it looks like," said Skye, opening his right arm up for me to join them.

I slid in front of Skye, and his body heat felt so wonderful, like the rising sun cracking ice in the early morning. I felt the heat spread through my chest as his body slowly warmed me. Wyatt still knelt near the tent door.

"Get over here, Wyatt," said Skye.

"I'm good. I'm warm enough."

"Dude. We want to live. Get in here, please. We're only thinking of survival. You of all people should get that."

Everything took a back seat to heat, to warmth, to living one more day, one more hour, one more minute.

Wyatt went over to Skye and scooted up next to him. "It's just to stay warm."

"No problems here, man," said Skye.

We rotated who was in the middle, so Wyatt eventually slid between me and Skye, and Shelby moved in front of me. Skye said he would stay on the outside, where the water was slowly dripping, because he was warm enough. I told him not to be a hero, but he said he was being honest. We always kept Nash at the very center.

Skye gave a small laugh. "You know, this may be the oddest human-interest piece Mrs. Wixom has ever seen. I'm going to write about this moment only. No context. No background or foreground or any ground but the tarp we're on and the dirt beneath."

"Edit for content," I said.

"Seems like everyone has stopped shivering," said Wyatt. "I'll go check on the raft in a second."

"We're trying some meditation to get our minds right," I said.

"We're warming up," said Skye, "but I wouldn't want to rush it. Best to stay like this for a few more hours."

Shelby laughed. I smiled and snuggled in closer to Skye.

"He's right. Best to be safe. Shelby knows I'm the best when it comes to bear hugs," I said. I pulled her closer, and she laughed again, her bald head right next to my nose. It smelled of sage and pine and sweat, though collectively we smelled of wet dog. Not a good mix.

We had water collecting nearby in the rain-fly. We hadn't found anything to catch the water in, so we'd angled the tarp to create a small pocket that would overflow but still hold water.

Wyatt spoke up. "When you're warm enough, step out and get a drink of water. We're losing a lot of good water, so better to drink it now and let it fill up again. Then come back and stay warm. I don't want anybody to panic."

"But what about getting to the cabin?" said Shelby. "What about our rescue?"

"We'll probably get help soon once the weather clears," said Wyatt. "Odds are, another outfit will pass us soon. We were pretty slow yesterday, and even slower today."

"And? What if we don't see another group?" I asked.

"Nash said bigger boats sometimes come up from the Sheep Creek Cabin area," said Wyatt. "And he said some people even have cabins there, so there must be people around."

"What if they're too busy staying warm inside their own tents?" said Skye.

"The crew will start searching for us once they see we're not at camp three. Which is looking more and more likely. Worst-case scenario, we don't get food until morning. Nash should last until then. We'll be okay," Wyatt said.

"Should?" I said.

"I'm not a doctor, Indie. But we also can't go back on the river in this weather."

Wyatt stood up and left us to check on the raft. I followed

him outside and hugged him from behind before he could make it very far.

"I'm glad you're here," I said.

It was maybe a little forward of me, but I didn't care.

"Me too," he said.

"Really?"

"Yeah. I'm glad I met you guys. Not for the whole almost-dying day, but the rest, of course."

"When do you think we can get back on the water?"

"Won't know until we know more."

"We should warm you up so you can English better."

He smiled. I got a drink from the fly and returned to the tent and snuggled up against Shelby.

"There are some traditions we should remember from this expedition," said Skye. "And I think those traditions will keep us close."

"Too close," said Shelby. "Don't tell anybody about this. Ever."

"I might let it slip," he said. "But what if we, like, made this a weekly thing? We can swim at Shelby's house in Jackson, and then retire to the pool house and snuggle instead of using towels."

"In your dreams," said Shelby.

"Yes. Yes, it will be in my dreams," said Skye.

It got quiet, and we were all tired and achy from the spill earlier and the resulting carnage, and I didn't want to speak or move or make any attempts at anything.

"This did help me forget about home, though," said Shelby. "And for that, I'm grateful."

"You have an amazing house," said Skye.

"You mean, *two* amazing houses," I said.

"But not a home," she said. "My parents only had me as a way of trying to keep the family together. Great idea, right? That always works. Except it didn't, so they split."

"Not your fault," said Skye.

"I know," she said. She was quiet for a minute. "Can I tell you guys something else? Sorry, talking helps me warm up and forget that I might die on this river."

I was breathing on Shelby's neck, Skye was on mine, and, later, Shelby and I rotated to remain warm. Nash was a boulder in the middle of the tent, his arm in a sling, his leg bent like some contortionist in the oddest of circumstances. I was starting to feel like I wanted an outside position in the odd Tootsie-Roll squeeze we had going on.

Wyatt unzipped the flap and hunched back into the tent. I could see out the door to the tree where Wyatt had tied our climbing rope to the raft to keep it in place. Much easier than dragging the raft up the slight incline in the dumping rain.

"So my mom got remarried to this jackwagon from Jackson," said Shelby. "They had a kid together, and I've been kind of, like, helping her out with stuff. Trying to be a good sister, I guess. A good *step*sister. But she has these tics because of her OCD. She'll alternate which eye blinks at which time, and she'll tap her foot in sets of three and clear her throat in sets of seven. It's so freaking weird."

"And you teased her about it?" I asked.

"No. Worse," Shelby said. "I was in Jackson with some friends, and they saw her and asked if she was my sister. And

I said I didn't know her, that she was a weirdo, and nobody I knew."

"Wow," said Wyatt.

"I know. I saw her tapping and blinking in patterns, and they all laughed, and I laughed with them and we walked away. I left her alone in the city center, even though she was just looking for someone to talk to who wouldn't judge her. And look at me: head smooth as a baby's bottom over here, judging others."

"To be fair," I said, "I thought Skye was going to be a stereotypical athlete. Eating raw meat and talking about hamstrings and stuff."

"Those are the two things you go to? Raw meat and hammies?" Wyatt said.

"I thought Wyatt was going to be super weird. I wasn't too far off," said Shelby.

"Aww, thanks, Shelbs," he said, reaching over to pat her arm.

The rain pattered. Our breathing fell in sync. Wyatt shifted. Skye moved his hand to my arm and squeezed. Shelby didn't say a word. None of us spoke for a moment.

"I'm sorry about Chisum," said Skye. "I mean it. I didn't know him, but what I did was wrong."

"You didn't know what they were planning," said Wyatt. "I believe you."

"Yeah, but that doesn't bring him back," said Skye. "And that's on me."

"That's not on you," said Wyatt.

"It's on all of us," I said. "Because stories are webs and not straight lines."

"What?" said Wyatt.

Skye squeezed my arm again, as if prompting me to continue.

"You're seeing the story move from A to B to C in a straight line, when in reality a great many strands came together to make Chisum's life the way it was. Yes, we can be better, but you can't blame yourself for what happened. You came in on one side of the web, and all the bullies came in on another. I can promise you that Chisum was thankful for having you as a friend."

"It's like light," said Shelby.

"What?" I said.

"Wyatt was talking about light earlier. I'm talking about lightness too, but the opposite of heavy, not the opposite of dark. All this crap at our feet is heavy. We make it light when we share it. I guess both meanings work. What is that, when the same word means different things?"

"Homonym," said Skye.

"Cheater. Did you read that on a cereal box?" said Wyatt.

"Ha ha," said Skye.

"Thanks for saying that, though, guys," said Wyatt. "But I can't bring Chisum back."

"And I can't make Nash take responsibility in that water instead of my mother, but I can forgive him. I guess that's like starting over, but I think it's more important to *continue*."

Skye squeezed my arm again and pulled me in a little closer.

"Speaking of Nash," said Wyatt. "I should probably get some water to give him some more pain meds. Don't want any of that pain coming back if we can keep it at bay."

The daylight was swallowed up in the rain, but there still existed a half-light through the pine trees that allowed for slight visibility beyond our location. I noticed this as Wyatt stepped outside the tent. But he didn't zip up the door, and I felt the cold sweep into the tent and stay, the wind whipping over my already chilly, goose-pimpled skin.

"Close the door, will you?"

I couldn't see Wyatt's eyes, but I saw his shoulders stiffen, and then we all heard his muttering turn into a moan and that moan turn into a scream that included many foul words. The exact words were muddled by the gargantuan drops of rain, but his tone was unmistakable.

My relationship with God was, at best, murky, and at worst, lost in some black hole beyond the reaches of the multiverse and all the theoretical physics and quantum mechanics my mother had studied. But that didn't mean I didn't still wonder about the timing of grand moments that seemed to awaken me to what I had and what I hadn't previously taken note of having. Like the rightness of having friends with me on this river trip where everything seemed to be wrong except for the group sharing all the wrongness with me.

Wyatt started moving frantically, and we sat up and looked past the small lip that curled from the bottom of the tent. Water was beginning to meet the threshold and spill into our tent, near the door. Wyatt stared at his feet as the water, filled with pine needles, rose to his ankles.

We were all so startled that, for a moment, nobody moved. Not until Skye got up and started cursing. Shelby and I followed him out of the tent.

Shelby stood with her hands over her ears and her eyes shut and started counting. None of us knew why. Then she jumped in the air and screamed as loud as anything I'd ever heard. Wyatt tried to get close, but she started swinging her arms until she reached twenty. Then, she stopped screaming and looked at us.

"I have to allow the freak-out if I'm going to get in that raft again. It's time to move. I'm not dying in hell."

"Okay," I said.

"Indie, help me with Nash," said Wyatt. "Shelby, Skye, pull the raft in using the climbing rope. Untie and collect the rope and hold the raft until we get there. Leave everything else. Put on your PFDs. Go. Now!"

Wyatt grabbed my arm and pulled me around Nash's side. The rising water had already pooled around Nash's body inside the tent. I leaned down and felt the soaked tent conform to my back as we both bent to pick up his limp body. We were moving too quickly for him to do anything more than groan and try to shift his weight off his leg.

I was thankful for the lightness of his body, relatively speaking. Nash was as thin as wallpaper and lanky and not much to carry, but it was still difficult because of the rapidly rising water. When we reached the raft, it was up to our knees.

Skye was already in the raft, and Shelby was standing with a loop in her hand, waiting for us.

"Grab him!" Wyatt yelled.

Skye helped take Nash's upper body, and Shelby climbed into the raft to help situate him into place. By the time I saw Wyatt roll himself into the raft, the water was closer to his waist than to his knees.

The storm was still dumping on us, like something biblical. The water rising in straight lines from the ripples on the surface was harrowing. The river had already exceeded its banks to the point that the river line was still noticeable, but it was so wide, I was unsure where to go.

The water had changed from a dark gray to a burnt orange. Debris floated by, and I saw a log as big as my trailer wash by us like it was weightless, humming along with such force that it took no care for any obstacle. I saw a smashed cooler float by, open and empty. As we hurtled forward, I saw an empty PFD, and my stomach turned. Who was without their vest? What company spilled? How many were lost in that orange, rising tide of water?

"We can't stay on the water. We need to get out of here. Scan the walls for any ledges. High ground. High ground!" Wyatt shouted.

I was focusing on the paddles, on keeping us from hitting any debris. Large fir trees and twisted pines rushed by, and I thought I heard in the distance a roar above and beyond the scream of water. We couldn't see the walls very well, so I knew I had to get us closer to the edge of the canyon before whatever it was I was hearing hit us.

And I knew we didn't have much time.

A clock ticked in my mind as I counted the trees passing us. I realized that our tents and our gear had probably washed away, lost in the churning water that was carrying giant boulders beneath us—boulders that hadn't moved in eons. I wondered about those prehistoric eggs and what dinosaurs had been freed from their burial in the map etched by the river over centuries.

"There!" Skye shouted, pointing, and I switched my control hand and pressed it against the flow to turn the raft eastward.

A plateau stuck out into the water like an arm, curling back into the wall, the color of Martian sand lit by some dying, red sun.

"Get the gear ready, Skye," said Wyatt. "I think the river is at its high point, but if not, we can't afford to lose anybody. We'll hold at that lip and see if we can place any climbing gear."

We had to shout to be heard above the rain and the great, heaving, panting beast of river upon whose back we were riding, the scales of the animal folding over one another in large pieces. Waves built foundations of massive buildings and then crumbled in an instant.

"How will we get Nash out?" I said.

"Z-pulley crevasse rescue," said Wyatt. "Maybe a drop loop assist."

"What does that mean?" said Shelby.

"That maybe we can do it," said Wyatt.

"Do we have the gear for that?" said Skye. "I haven't climbed since I lost my leg. I don't think we can manage with his weight, Wyatt. I hate this thing!" Skye started punching his prosthetic, and the skin on his knuckles tore open.

I saw tears in his eyes. Or was that just the rainwater?

"Dammit, Skye, I know you can climb," said Wyatt.

"I used to climb," he said. "Now I just tie knots and sit. I'm useless."

"Well, Nash lives or dies depending on your decision," said Wyatt. "So don't take too long to make up your mind."

Skye rubbed his hand against his thigh.

"I know you can do this, Skye," Wyatt said again.

"We could lash the oars together and tie him down to that. Would that work?" I asked.

"He needs to use his other leg and arm. If he can't help himself, we can't make it up that wall," said Wyatt.

We were twenty yards from the outcropping Skye had spotted. It was noticeable, even in the half-light of dusk, because of the way the dark rocks near the edge reached out into the canyon like dirty fingers on an otherwise clean hand, a hand that connected to that red-armed plateau. The rock surrounding the plateau looked like bright, sheer limestone; it set the ledge in relief.

The ledge was a couple feet from the boat, and I did what I could to hold the raft as close to it as possible. Wyatt climbed out and pulled himself up. He yelled to Skye for the rope and a cam with a quickdraw attached. Skye threw him the gear, and we sat in an eddy that seemed to rise like a blister with every passing second. But it lifted us up enough that we could step out onto the plateau with more confidence.

"Put on a harness!" Wyatt yelled. "Hurry up!"

Somehow, Wyatt found an opening for the climbing cam, and the cam opened up in the wall and held, like a muscle flexing behind the stone. He clipped the rope in, tied it around his body, and leaned over the edge to help the rest of us up to a rim above the plateau, more than two feet above the rising water.

The roar of water I'd heard earlier seemed to be increasing, and I doubted any of us would make it out of that spot, no matter the rope, the cams, the quickdraws, the oars or the PFDs or the raft or anything. But that didn't stop me from trying.

Another raft slid onto the plateau as if arriving from some

other world. The five people in it jumped out and ran to the wall. They all looked to be in their thirties or older, and each one had on a PFD and was panting heavily. I assumed the man with the bandana on his head was the guide by the way his face contorted into a frown. He held the raft next to him by the guide rope and stood with his back to the wall.

"Do you have enough equipment to get us all out?" he said.

"We have the gear, but I don't know how much time we have," said Skye.

"We'll get everyone out. Help us clip this guy in and get him into a position where he can get himself up the wall," said Wyatt.

Skye handed me the second harness and told me to put it on and strap down. I moved as quickly as possible. Skye tied a rope around Nash, and Wyatt pulled on Shelby's PFD and rolled her closer to the wall.

There was not enough room on the ledge for all of us, so the other company stood near the wall on the plateau, the water up to their knees. Maybe it was a trick of my eyes, but it seemed like the water wasn't rising as fast as it had before.

"Hurry!" said Wyatt.

"Shut up! I am!" said Skye.

Nash tried to lift his body to make it easier for Skye to get the rope around him, but the movement made him scream in pain. The wind blew everybody's hair into their faces, and I could barely see Nash's face beneath the white mop of his beard.

Skye had tied the rope around Nash's waist and through his legs multiple times, knotting it near his belly button. Skye then handed me the other side of the climbing rope and released the loop he'd tied into. Wyatt reached down to help move me closer to Shelby, creating enough room for one of the other company to stand on the ledge.

"Get the Z-pulley ready!" Skye shouted to Wyatt, and I leaned over to help Skye.

Skye tied into the anchor and clipped his carabiner into the line to create two alpine loops for me and Shelby. He put a carabiner on Shelby's PFD and clipped her in along with Wyatt. Had we more time, I would have gladly switched places with Wyatt and given him the harness. Nash's leg was too mangled to get a harness on him, and we were praying the rope would hold.

Wyatt placed another cam in the wall and made sure Shelby and I were secure. I checked the knot, and then tried to help Skye get Nash closer to the wall.

But we didn't have time to get him to the wall or say the prayers we'd been hoping to say, because a giant wave of water was upon us. A deafening roar, like a jet engine, split the sky and rushed past us like a fierce wind, and then the water pulled Nash away and the rest of us with him.

The other company clung to the wall as the water hit them. One of the four men standing next to the guide slipped past the ledge and was gone, a dot in the water, vanishing beyond the orange waves. His screams, and the screams of his friends, were swallowed by the deafening roar from the water.

Skye was in water up to his waist and trying to keep his footing. The other guide and his group began free solo climbing as high as they could next to us, crimping, keeping their bodies close to the wall, their faces pressed against the rock and their eyes closed against the spray from the water. Another of their group slipped and grabbed Nash's body in the process.

Shelby and Wyatt were both holding onto the cams, their bodies sliding horizontally from the thrash of the water, the surge of the flood.

I saw Nash's body begin to slip from the rope, so I created slack in the line and, without thinking, I dove for him. The water was pulling him away and his hands were reaching out and his face was underwater, like some demented swimmer with no way to kick, no way to advance.

A log riding the water missed me by a few feet but knocked into Nash's leg, propelling us both out farther from Skye. That same log took another rafter with it. The other company was down to three people, including the guide.

I grabbed onto Nash's shoulder on his good arm and tried to find his hand, but his hand found my necklace first. The chain popped, and I felt the release of it as I swung my other arm to grab Nash's hand.

Skye was horizontal in the raging current, and we all attempted to keep our heads above the water, our feet downstream, as Wyatt and Shelby worked on pulling us back in.

The raft was miles down what seemed to be a mile-wide river.

Along with my mother's ring.

I couldn't think about what I'd lost when Nash pulled on my necklace, only the fact that he wasn't lost.

The wall of water that wiped away our raft, and had almost taken Nash with it, had also been the last surge of water from what seemed an inexhaustible glut of water from the silver sky above.

Darkness continued to descend as Nash and I slowly approached the wall in short bursts of swimming. Skye, who was now at the wall and hooked into a cam, shouted at me to swim hard, and then he'd cinch off the rope on his belay device and wait for me to rest before another try.

After three more sharp bursts of energy, I was only a few feet away from the wall, and Skye was able to pull me in. Nash stayed in the water while Skye, Wyatt, and Shelby worked to set up the Z-pulley. I held Nash close to me as Skye shouted that he would be climbing ten feet above and setting up our exit, the pulley, our rescue.

What felt like an hour had only taken a few minutes.

"You didn't hesitate, Indie," Nash said, coughing out water.

"What?"

"No hesitation. Just like your mother."

Nash looked like he'd aged ten years, and I was sure I looked as awful and haggard, but it didn't matter. In that moment, I built a church in my heart for my mother. A sanctum to honor those lost and those found.

What I hadn't noticed until we were closer to the wall and hugging the rock were the waterfalls that were spouting off the canyon rim and into the river. What I'd taken for crazy amounts of rain turned out to be water rushing from the canyon cliffs above.

I was cold and alive and thankful to be feeling cold and alive. My arms were numb. My feet were numb. My face had little to no feeling. My hands were almost nonresponsive. My injured arm was still throbbing, Wyatt's makeshift bandage long since gone, but I kept holding onto Nash.

Shelby had worked another cam into the wall, though it didn't look very sturdy. The guide from the other group had ripped the rope from their raft's outer rim and clipped it into our rope. If he fell, at least we could keep him and the two others from floating into oblivion. Maybe.

And Nash was right. I hadn't hesitated. I reached for him instead of the necklace, and I didn't think twice about the choice I was making.

Because even those we once hated can show us how to love. Because choices will always exist, and when they present themselves, I hope to always reach for the right hand. Because forgiveness is the real river we run in this life.

TEN

It's no use going back a day or two or ten, because I was a different person then. I knew who I was when I got in that hearse with Grandpa and made my way to Hells Canyon, but I wasn't so sure I knew who I was when I jumped in the river for Nash. Or maybe I didn't know who I was when I got in that hearse, and I finally found myself in my leap for Nash. I couldn't explain it myself because I wasn't acting like myself. My selfhood was no longer a part of me. It had detached and floated down the river, and I'd become this new thing, this new person, this new being who would leap into the void for somebody I once hated. I didn't know who I was.

Not anymore. The energy I'd kept coiled within my chest had whispered out of my body like a breath and vanished into that canyon. All the anger and hate I'd kept for Nash was gone, like I'd finally opened the cage and let the animal loose. That cage had rattled for two years, my fingers white from gripping the lock, but the feeling was beginning to come back to them now that I'd finally released it and let the thing swing open.

I thought of this as I stared at Wyatt and Skye while they

helped Nash into a stable position in a chimney rock formation they'd found. We left him there until we figured out how to help the other guide and the two rafters with him climb up onto the lip near the plateau, where they could finally rest their hands after crimping for ten minutes, hugging the wall with their fingertips.

And then the most beautiful thing I'd ever seen in my life happened: a full moon pushed its way through the silver clouds, and a black sky began to materialize in place of the thunderheads. Stars scattered above like a billion holes in a piece of black paper or a sheet of corrugated tin set to the light. The stars were center stage, like they'd been waiting in the wings until the flood passed so they could hog the spotlight.

The river was receding, but slowly. It was still roiling beneath the crag, but we were focused on setting cams in the wall and figuring out if we had enough gear to make it to the canyon rim.

Fortunately, from where we were, the wall didn't seem to be as high as I'd once thought. Or it could have been the fact that anything short of Everest looked like a day in Bali after surviving a flash flood. Either way, we mapped out an exit route just in case the clouds decided to change course. Again.

"I've never been so thankful for light," I said.

"Me neither," said Shelby. "Good homonym, though. I like it."

She was resting against the rock with her foot in a jug the size of Texas. Having both of us standing on the lip meant the three others below us could keep the entire ledge to themselves, even though it was still a tight squeeze.

Above us, Skye worked on placing more gear in the wall on the outside of the chimney. Wyatt belayed Skye using the harness I'd been wearing earlier. Using some webbing from our guide rope, the guys hooked Nash into the wall to help him stay semi-secure.

We both stood against the wall, leaning our weight into the rock, and I rested my head on Shelby's shoulder.

"Can we still be friends after all of this?"

"I think that's part of the whole we-almost-died contract," she said. "Like, it's written into the thing. No way out of it, now."

"And you'll forget what a jerk I was to Nash? And you? How I brooded for, like, days?"

"That wasn't brooding. Come over to my house, and I'll show you how to really brood. Wait till my stepfather walks into a room, and I'll show you how it's done. I'll freaking brood you out of your mind. I'll brood up a storm." She grinned. "But that means you have to forget about my bald head."

"Shut up. It looks great. I meant what I said. I wish I could pull that off."

Above us, Wyatt pulled in and cinched the rope at his ATC before letting out more as Skye clambered up the wall. I heard the rope zip past a carabiner, and the distinct clip of the quick-draw that followed before Skye shouted, "Take!"

Wyatt eased back into his harness and set his feet on the rock, waiting for Skye to climb on.

Perhaps because of what we'd been through that day, the idea of climbing seventy feet out of the canyon didn't seem to faze us. If we got out of the canyon, even without food or water or shelter, I felt we'd be safe. Something about rising above those towering walls made me feel hopeful and light.

"What are you going to write your feature piece on?" I asked Shelby.

"Seriously? Right now? You want to talk about school?"

"No. I want to talk about something to keep from thinking of how we're not back home or anywhere near school. Because school is safe. Easy. Warm."

"That's fair," she said.

"You know, I was all set on writing about tourism ruining the environment. Like, really sticking it to this outfit and others like it because of what happened to my mom. But now, I don't know what to write about."

"I'm going to write mine on being hairless."

"No more wigs at school?"

"Nope."

"Hairless and careless. Carefree, more like it," I said.

"What's yours gonna be on, then?" she said, resting her head on mine in turn.

"Not sure yet."

"You know, good stories remind us what it means to be. To exist."

"And good reporting?" I said.

"Same thing. It's not about sending a message about *your* world; it's about writing articles so people recognize it's *our* world."

"We're in this together," I said.

"Yep."

At that moment, Wyatt zipped down the rope and released

tension and shouted to Skye. Shelby and I stood up, and I felt my muscles retract and the ache return. My left knee was pulsing with pain on either side of the kneecap, and I wasn't sure if something was torn or pulled or strained or yanked or snapped. I wasn't sure of much.

They'd set up a top-rope climb and tied into a tree on the rim of the canyon with the cut-up webbing of the old guide rope from the raft. Nash was already up top. Wyatt was out of breath and leaning into the wall.

"Time to climb," said Wyatt.

"Shelbs first," I said. "I mean, Shelby."

"Shelbs is okay, but only with you guys. Not at school."

"Shelbs it is," I said.

"I don't know if I can do this, guys," she said. "I'm afraid of heights. I've never even been climbing except for when we rappelled into this stupid canyon. This is ridiculous."

Wyatt put the harness on Shelby and tied the figure-eight knot, then traced it back and tugged on it as she continued to fret.

"Did you see any other outfits?" Shelby said to the three guys below us as Wyatt secured her harness.

The guide looked up, the moon reflecting in his dark eyes, and brushed his hair back. "We saw one flipped raft, and one jet boat sinking. There is one other party up a ways tied to a tree, but I don't know if there's any other way out. We can't risk another earth dam breaking and taking us with it."

"Only one way out, Shelbs," said Wyatt, tugging on the rope.

"Up," I said.

My voice echoed, and I wondered if that echo would ever escape the canyon walls. *Up.* I didn't want to make Shelby more anxious, so I didn't mention the fact that we had to hurry. Nobody knew what the clouds were going to do, and I wasn't ready for another wall of water to rip through the canyon.

Shelby was a decent climber, despite her reservations. She was all arms, typical of a rookie, but Wyatt coached her through it and helped her find the large features and footholds.

Thirty minutes later, Shelby was up top with Nash and Skye, and the rope was back, attached to the harness, for me.

"Easy climb," Wyatt said. "You can do this in half the time it took Shelbs. Lots of big jugs. Not a joke about anatomy, just a climbing term."

"I know how to climb," I said. "And I know that jugs are easiest to grab."

I had to focus on my footing even with the large jugs—my arms were torn up, and my shoulders were particularly sore from my work with the oars. Thankfully, with a top-rope climb, a lot of work was done by Wyatt cinching off on his ATC with my every move and counterbalancing with his weight.

He pulled me up the wall more than I climbed it, really. At least it felt that way. He made quick work of helping the other three guys up the wall, and we got them safely out of the canyon. When the other guide topped out, I used my own belay device to help Wyatt up the wall. He climbed it in half the time I had. He made it look easy. I was impressed he still had enough energy to scamper like that.

When Wyatt got to the top, I set the rope out next to Nash, who was hunched and groaning from the pain. Shelby was flat on her back and had removed her PFD, her chest rising and falling in the moonlight. Skye was looking into the distance, where the mountain features bled into the dark-blue starlit sky and then into the black. The other three guys were huddled near a twisted pine tree, shivering and clinging to their PFDs.

It felt like it was fifty degrees outside, and before the adrenaline finished its course in our systems, Wyatt shouted at us to remove our PFDs and huddle up.

"Not this again," said Shelby.

"Only way to stay warm," he said, sidling up to Shelby. Skye followed shortly thereafter, and I rushed to bear hug Shelby as well.

"Fair enough," said Shelby. "I guess with what we've been through, no amount of snuggling theatrics would surprise me anyway."

Shelby started laughing, and we all joined in, feeling this odd release of tension, because even if the clouds returned and the rain picked back up—even then—we'd be free of the massive canyon walls and the way they leaned over us and stared at us. Oh, and the crushing rapids, of course. I'd never been so happy to be clear of a river. Usually, I was aching to get near the water, to cast a line and see what was biting.

We huddled together for what seemed like another hour, sleeping in fits and starts, like the sound of birdsong in the morning. Nash's breathing slowed, and he repeated the same thing over and over: "I'm sorry, team." That word, *Sorry*. A word I once leaned on without understanding its power, its bearing-wall strength. But I knew he did, and it had cost him more than I'd first imagined.

Wyatt was checking Nash's pulse with his fingers on his neck and looking at his arm and leg when I heard the most beautiful sound. No, it wasn't the river. No, it wasn't the osprey sending its call out into the night or the bald eagle calling back. It was the sound of a helicopter in the distance, all those blades cutting the nighttime sky, *thwump-thwump-thwumping* in the blackness.

I thought I saw a spotlight in the distance, but I wasn't sure until the light washed over us, and the helicopter drew close to our position and hovered. A rescue worker lowered an odd combination of a stretcher and a cage attached to his rope, and one by one, we each rose into the sky, into safety, into a world apart from the arms of water still thrashing below, still reaching for us, still opening and closing in rage.

The blades turned overhead, and the sound boomed, drowning out any other noise. Skye scooted closer, and the wool blanket around his shoulders scratched at my frozen cheeks.

I reached for my necklace only to grasp nothing, and remembered that somewhere below, in the pull of the river, the ring was caught beneath the deep blue rapids where shimmering fish darted. I tasted salt in my mouth. I feared the heaviness in my gut might take hold of me and sink me through the floor of the helicopter and back into the canyon, to be washed away like the ring.

Skye pulled me into his body, and I felt the warmth from his chest soak into my cold frame. The idea of returning to school and seeing Skye there and being part of a different group and having friends who knew me—like, *really* knew me—gave me hope.

Certain things, certain people, once known, cannot be un-known or escaped. Nor would I want to escape that. That hope burst like millions of stars in my mind as my body sank into a slump. The stars blurred beyond the helicopter's windshield. I gazed in silence and began to doze. I didn't need the movement of the helicopter to lull me—I was already exhausted. I shifted my weight, and I fell asleep against Skye as the nighttime stars continued to burn before the helicopter, unmoved.

≈

When I woke in the hospital, there were no other beds in my room. I saw options appear before me, which meant I was probably still alive.

1. *Start screaming hysterically until a nurse arrives. Ask for some Jell-O and a TV remote and binge-watch HGTV.*
2. *Sleep for another week.*
3. *Ask for a wheelchair. Practice wheelies in the hallway.*
4. *Find the others immediately.*

I considered number 2 briefly, but ended up going with number 4. I did call for a nurse, but only to ask for a wheelchair. The nurse told me I should stay in my room and rest under the weighted blankets, but I was already sweating so much that damp tacos had formed under my arms. I told her I needed to cool down a bit and got out of bed.

I wheeled myself down the hallway to Shelby's room. The fluorescent lights pooled and reflected off the laminated tile. It was a depressing glimmer, but I wasn't feeling depressed.

Once the nurse had gone, I climbed out of the wheelchair

and jumped into bed with Shelby. Her head popped up in surprise.

"You scared the crap out of me," she said.

"I don't see a colostomy bag."

"Gross."

"Not even a catheter," I said.

"Just glad we have a real bathroom here instead of that stupid groover. They must trust us to go by ourselves."

"Speaking of going," I said, "how long do you think they are going to keep us here?"

Shelby shifted in the bed and pressed the button that lifted the entire upper half slowly to a sitting position with a humming whir.

"Long enough," she said.

"So profound. Have you checked on the others?"

"Seriously? I just woke up."

"Just checking. Got a TV remote?" I asked.

"Slow down. I'm still headachy."

"Your head is the only reason we're safe," I said.

"What?"

"Well, it's not like we had any reflectors on our vests, right?"

"So?"

"So that spotlight had to hit something."

Shelby smiled and punched me in the arm.

I hopped off her bed and back into the wheelchair. I called for the nurse to help me find the other rooms that my friends were in.

When we got to the next room, I wheeled in as the nurse

walked to a desk to talk with a couple other nurses, probably to tell them how awful I was as a patient.

I wheeled past the curtain hanging halfway to the floor and saw Skye and Wyatt on the couch covered in a couple blankets. Nash had his own bed, his leg and arm both wrapped, an IV dripping into his arm.

"Shelby and I got our own suites. How'd you guys end up on the couch?"

"Are you feeling okay, Indie?" said Nash.

"I'm fine."

"Are you sure?"

"Nash has been asking about you. He's nothing if not concerned," said Skye.

I saw a couple half-eaten meals on small tables. From the angle of the sun, I assumed it was past noon, but I was unsure how long I'd been out.

"This was my fault, team," Nash said.

"Pretty sure it wasn't," said Wyatt, turning up the volume on the TV burbling overhead.

A talking head appeared, of course. She was beautiful and had massive teeth and huge eyes and was overly expressive. She was perfect for TV—and probably great at charades, too. That was my first thought, anyway. But all my other thoughts, from second to seventieth, followed her reporting as different images from Hells Canyon flitted across the screen.

Twenty-seven dead. Six were students visiting from various schools. Two of those had worked for Jet Boat River Tours to earn some summer cash for school. Abbey Outdoor Pursuits lost ten people to the flood. Edmund Hillary Adventures lost seven. There were three family members staying in a cabin just one mile from our last camp—they were gone. The cabin itself had been washed away completely. There were still four missing, according to the reporter, though apparently four of the five people tied to the tree had made it out alive. We watched recorded coverage of their helicopter rescue.

Images of a boulder-choked region of the canyon reappeared, showing massive logs that had been swept into walls and splintered by the force of impact. The Sheep Creek Cabin site was shown multiple times, empty, soaked and torn and shot through with mud and covered with a field of newly placed, newly *left* boulders. The newscaster cut between reporters wearing slickers and numerous interviews. Every channel seemed to have another meteorological expert, local outfitter, or dam engineer talking into a microphone.

The concrete gravity dam on the Idaho–Oregon border had burst because of the sheer strength of the downpour. Footage of the aftermath was shown on a loop—massive slabs of concrete slotted against one another or pressed up into felled pines, their mangled rebar insides reaching into the open sky. Giant cuts of the rock tilted sideways in heavy, wet mud.

The river had dropped considerably, but it would take years before the total weight of the slide, of the break, could be adequately measured. Sections of road near the dam had been washed away completely, asphalt crumbling into the clay beneath street level. Yellow police tape crisscrossed each scene like some crude version of graveyard markers. Helicopters whirred overhead, *thwumping* high and dropping rescue workers and ropes into the canyon.

One woman had been pulled from a tree five miles beyond where we climbed out, which turned out to be ten miles beyond the Sheep Creek Cabin site where we had planned to stop. I wondered if she was the other rafter from the group we climbed out with, the one who fell into the water after we lost the one to the log. How much was underwater by the time we climbed out?

The weather service had received reports of shifting systems too late in the game. Had they known earlier, we would have been pulled by rescue teams on the second day of the trip. But even knowing about the storm wouldn't have prepared them for the dam break. "Intermittent showers were reported in some cities along the canyon," the newscasters kept repeating. "But never thunderstorms."

The water rose 0.8 cubic meters per second, according to a hydrologist with the US Army Corps of Engineers in Washington. The engineer explained that meant more than two hundred gallons of water rose in that river per second—an amount that multiplied exponentially when the dam burst.

It was a disaster of epic proportions. It demonstrated starkly to all of us a river's strength and how it can move and what it can take. But also the strength of people, and what they can survive.

The flood hadn't descended as a massive wall, which allowed some groups, like ours, to clamber onto ledges or outcroppings or even into trees, said one reporter. Many, unsure if the water would continue to rise, swam to banks and attempted to climb out. Most didn't make it.

Twenty-seven dead. The number repeated in my mind as I

rested my hand on the cool curve of the wheelchair and pivoted to see the faces of the others, which were glued to the screen above. I hadn't heard or noticed that Shelby had walked in and was now standing behind me.

"Unreal," she said.

"Exactly," said Wyatt.

"Glad you guys know how to climb. We're lucky," said Nash. "If not for you, we'd all be goners. I didn't help that."

He looked up at the TV screen, his eyes full. He looked so much weaker under the artificial lighting of the hospital room. His tanned arms looked frail, his face sunken and tired. We were probably going against all orders by being in the room with him, or even out of our own beds.

"You didn't cause *that*," I said, pointing at the screen above our heads.

A disaster that had garnered national attention, and probably would for weeks. For months. As I stared at the figures on the screen, I thought about how we all start out life with a pocketful of coins and we determine how those are spent. I'd been flipping mine into the river, into boxes of memory, neat packages of an edited past, into a blue-dark pit of shame and grief and anger and hatred and resentment, when I should have been investing them in new friends.

I thought of that coin I'd wedged into the asphalt before joining the group that first day. I understood, now, after our hellacious canyon trip, that those investments would continue to offer returns, to fill up the bank, to make my pockets overflow for the rest of my life.

The nurse came in to wheel me back to my room. I hugged

my friends, one by one, until I felt that things were getting a bit too chummy, a bit too sentimental for my liking.

"Meet in Shelbs's room when you can," said Skye in a whisper.

I nodded and was about to leave, but when I saw Nash, I hesitated.

"It's over. We did it. We ran the river," I said.

"Or it ran us," he said, smiling.

"Mom would be proud of you," I said. "She always did like you."

He waved his good arm in a modest "get out of here" gesture.

"And I think I know why, now. And I want you to know that, well, it's okay," I said.

"It's okay?"

"Yeah. It's okay. I meant it on the river. I mean it now."

"Thank you, Indie." Nash shifted in his bed and tried to adjust his arm with little success. "You're a lot like your mom. Stubborn, smart, and lots of grit. Thanks for not giving up on me."

"Don't give up on yourself."

"I'll try not to," he said.

"You should move back, you know," I said. "Home."

"I know," he said, picking at the IV in his arm. "I just couldn't stand looking up the hill to Tetonia and knowing I'd taken her from you."

"Everyone wants forgiveness of some sort, but everyone refuses to believe in mercy," I said.

"What's that?"

"Something Grandpa always says." I watched as an

accordion of starlings expanded and retracted outside the hospital window.

"Thank you, Indiana," he said, his eyes full.

"For what? I'm talking about both of us," I said. "Because I needed your forgiveness just as much. I know that now."

"You always had it," he said. "Anyway, I'm just glad I got to be your guide."

I imagined some Hallmark film, where the girl hears such a comment and says "Or was I your guide?" and then they both break down and sob and go through photo albums together. But it wasn't like that, because that's not real life.

"Heading back after this?" I asked.

"Might go to Henry's and drop a line with some old friends while I'm close by. See if I can't fish with only one arm."

"Browns are hungry. Make sure if you get a rainbow that you let it run."

"I always do," he said.

Let it run. Let the fish run. When you hook a fish, you let it run and feel free before yanking the barb and reminding it that it cannot leave your line. It then knows its place. Small amounts of freedom make it so it won't yank too hard and rip off the hook. Letting the fish run allows for a slower but more sure catch. When those rainbows dive, you got to let them think they're in charge before you hand that rod to God.

I walked out of Nash's room, and I found myself floating, almost. Forgiveness was offered and accepted, and I was now the other self, a carefree person without a chip on her shoulder, without a wedge in her heart, without a rip in her chute. I was floating back down to earth instead of plummeting into a river of grief.

All rivers change direction and cut through rocks—rocks with raindrops etched into them from the beginning of time, rocks as old as humankind. There are no set limits on how a river runs, or where, or why, or when it will cut through those ancient rocks, where words have been hiding since the world first turned. Those words will break free at some point, and they will remind us that life is a way of loving, not a set of rules.

The nurse wheeled me out of Nash's room despite my hearty protests. I shouted to the others that I would meet them later in Shelbs's room. When I got to my room, the nurse said I had to stay put for a half hour so the doctor could clear me. I stared out the window while I waited, catching a slight shimmer from the Snake River in the distance.

I would never go to Hells Canyon again, I knew that much, but I was still happy to see the river, to live near a stretch of river that I knew as well as Bury's face in the morning light that peeked through our shabby trailer curtains. I could name every turn and hollow of that river, every tree and dip. I could probably give the exact number of rocks rollicking around the bottom of the Snake River if I had to.

"That's a good sign," said Skye.

I turned and saw him standing in my doorway.

"What?"

"The cattle out there. They're standing. That means the water's fishy and the fish are biting. If the cattle are lying down, it means the fish aren't going to bite."

"Fishermen and their superstitions," I said. "Speaking of, I notice you haven't been touching your leg as much today."

He touched his prosthetic reflexively, his face turning red. "It's become sort of a safety net thing. I do it when I'm anxious."

"Why are you anxious?"

"I told you on the river," he said.

"I don't remember."

"It's because I don't really know what to do with my life now. Well, I didn't. I've only ever known soccer, and now that's gone. I keep worrying about who I used to be and feeling anxious about who I'm supposed to be now. Stupid, I know."

"Not stupid. And? You said *didn't*, right?"

"Right. I really want to guide like my dad. Fly-fishing. It's what I love."

"Your dad will be okay with that?" I asked.

"Who cares?"

"You're right," I said.

"It's what I want to do. I just didn't know it until I was without soccer and only had a fly-rod in my hand and nobody to tell me what to do or how to do it. I didn't know what I needed until we dropped into hell. Take that for a Sunday sermon, amirite?"

Skye walked in and sat down next to me in the sunlight I was soaking up.

"Makes me wonder what secrets my mom was keeping," I said, slouching back into the uncomfortable, hospital-grade couch and staring out the window at the cattle near the river. "Or Grandpa. Hell, everybody. We all think we have to carry the weight alone, too."

"I lied to you," said Skye, staring out the window.

I turned to face him. "What?"

"The alert I got when I was driving? I told everyone it was just a text."

"What was it?" I asked.

"You'll think I'm a nerd," he said.

"I sure hope so."

"It was an alert from *Science Daily*. I've been interested in stuff like that since your mom's class."

"So what was it? No way you forgot that alert."

"Never."

"And?"

"It was an article about why space is so dark," said Skye.

"Okay. I'm listening," I said.

"We only see light in space when it hits an object and bounces off it."

I stared at the light hitting the cattle, the shadows at their feet, the darkness around them.

"That's so cool," I said. "Life is always dark until we bounce off each other."

"Light?"

"Life. I said *life*. It takes other people. That's the only way to be seen."

Wyatt walked in with Shelby, and they both sat next to Skye, so close that Skye winced and stood up.

"Sure. Have a seat."

"Thanks, man," said Wyatt, smiling.

"I'm trying to not say that anymore," said Skye.

"You can still say it. But you and I will know it's for ironic purposes only," Wyatt said.

"Fair enough," said Skye.

"You think you're ready for your big coming-out party?" Wyatt said, pointing at Skye's prosthetic. We all smiled and looked at Wyatt, who had a too-big grin on his face, smiling at the kernel of his own corny humor. A homophone I knew they'd appreciate some other time.

"I'll be okay. You ready for yours? I imagine coming out won't be easy."

"Staying out is even more difficult. But I'm going to bring down the house, man," said Wyatt. "Just you watch."

"Now you're talking," said Skye.

"I've been talking this whole time," said Wyatt.

"You both talk a lot," said Shelby.

I guess we all meet that second person who is inside of us, eventually. I wondered how I was like Skye and Wyatt and Shelby. They all lived with a duality, and it made sense that they could live their lives as more than one thing. We all had secrets that needed extra hands to carry, lives that needed that river run, darkness that needed light, weight that needed lightness.

It felt odd to feel like myself again, there in that moment with those three people. I mean, I almost didn't recognize the spunk that reappeared in me after the river, after I met Skye and Wyatt and Shelby. It's like I had ignored my personality for so long after my mom died that it was packing up and getting ready to leave, to trot off, for good. I was lucky it hadn't gotten too far before these friends helped me beckon it back with corny jokes and hearse puns with Grandpa.

I heard a nurse complaining in the hallway about how dogs were not allowed in the hospital, but Bury was on me before Grandpa could finish arguing. He shouted something about how he'd take care of it, and then walked in, hat in hand, eyes full. He looked tired as well, worn, tattered, his sweatshirt a threadbare version of what once had probably offered a good deal of warmth.

"Lucky as the day is long," he said, almost swallowing the last half of the sentence in tears.

"Grandpa," I said.

I hugged him and felt his body slacken and his chest heave as he worked to hold back the tears. Bury leapt onto me again, her massive paws covering my chest, and started licking my face. I fell to the ground and rolled around with her and hugged her so tight she squirmed to get free.

"I missed you, Bury."

Grandpa laughed. "Wish I got half the greeting that dog gets. You're not allowed to leave Tetonia again. Not until you're forty-five."

"Arbitrary pick. Why forty-five?"

"I don't know. Just gives me a lot of time with you and fewer worries."

"If I can't leave Tetonia, we won't have groceries."

"We'll live off the land. I have a few rifles."

"Black powder?"

"Your jokes about my age get worse and worse, Indie. I hope she wasn't this unkind on the river," he said to my friends.

Wyatt, Skye, and Shelby just smiled.

Grandpa laughed as I stood up and stuck his hat back on his head.

"We'll let you two go," said Wyatt.

They all stood, and we hugged before they stepped into the light pooling in the hospital's overly-large white hallway. I watched them leave, then turned to Grandpa. He handed me a bag, and I went to the bathroom to change. Of course, the clothes he brought turned out to be about five years past their wearable date.

As we walked out into the arms of a quiet, open sky, I joked, "You couldn't bring me some sweats or something?"

"I was in a hurry. Just sit back and calm down," he said, followed by a laugh through his nostrils.

"What's so funny?"

"Nothing," he said.

"What?"

"You just survived a flash flood, and you're complaining about your clothing. It's such a small, silly worry in light of what you've been through. Reminds me of rearranging deck chairs on the *Titanic*, is all."

"Huh. I guess you were at about the right age to be working on that boat," I said.

"Should've left you in that hospital."

"Missed opportunities, right?"

Bury ran to the black car reflecting the afternoon light.

"You brought the hearse? Also, can I note that no normal teenager should have to ever speak that sentence in their life? And I just did."

"Everyone wants to ride in it. It's a gift that keeps on giving."

"Everyone gets that ride—eventually. But I wouldn't call it a gift," I said.

"That's not what I was saying," said Grandpa.

"Ah, but it's what I was saying. I said it, therefore I was saying it."

"You're impossible."

"Only if you believe I am," I said.

"You're also crazy."

"All the best people are."

"Right. Get into the hearse. It's a good car—it has proper heating and good shocks and struts. Just don't complain."

"No complaints here."

I sat back and listened to the *snicker-snack* of the shocks and struts as they jounced in rhythm with the pocked road as we worked our way through the large valleys at the base of the Teton range.

Old ranches sat heavy with dilapidated silos. Tractors taking their last breath of summer sat next to rusted washing machines and worn saddles ripped by the seasons into tattered memories of summer days. Cattle slouched in the fields. Short-shadowed horses stood still in a wind that carried dandelion seeds for miles.

I rested my head against the window and watched the land scroll by. I admired the purple shadows hitting the vast expanse of the Teton Mountains as we turned down the road leading to Victor. I looked to the white clouds settling over our small town. We passed the Victor Post, Barbecue Hole, the Knotty Pine Bar, and the Fin and Feather Inn. Beyond those establishments sat the cemetery, and in that cemetery was a grave with my mother's name on it. I reached to my chest again, force of habit, and remembered what was not there anymore, and thought of what had taken its place.

Grandpa said he would have been at the hospital sooner, but he had been working with the backhoe to keep the cemetery half-in-place after the thunderbumpers made their way through Victor. I knew the next few weeks, even months, would be spent with Grandpa, working a skid-steer and backhoe, trying to repair stretches of the cemetery and the crumbling asphalt paths that had been completely washed away. I also knew half the town would help, bringing their own winches and tractors and shovels, and getting things back to normal—whatever that meant.

"Uncomely as a drove of pigs," said Grandpa.

"But it pays the bills, right?" The cemetery looked like a set of teeth with canines missing.

"My poker pays the bills. That gets me a tax write-off on the hearse. I guess it's worth it, though. It may be as big as a boardinghouse dumpling, but it works. Can't argue with that. Well."

And that single word—*Well*—summed up all of his frustration coupled with his relief that I was still there to talk to him instead of needing my own plot of ground.

I stared at Grandpa's stoic profile. He was my rock, my boulder, and even with all the storms and rain and hail beating down upon him, all the currents circling and pushing and pulling, I knew he'd never move. He'd remain that rock in my life until the world stopped turning.

As we turned just beyond Victor, a drift boat happened by in the distance, lines swirling over heads, flies hopping near the water.

Catch and release. It was written into my blood.

Grandpa would often speak to the rainbows wimpling in the river ten yards from the shore, twisting in the cool current. He'd talk to the fish and tell it all about the fly sitting on the seam and how he'd spent a long time making it look just right, and that he was only after a closer look at the patterns on its sides, of its colorful scales winking in the water, and that then he'd return it back to the water. I would laugh, but Grandpa would just continue talking to the fish. He would say, "Sorry, fella" to the fish, and release it back into that river full of sky. It was that easy.

I watched those rods move in the evening light and thought of Wyatt. And Shelby. And Skye. I watched the river run through our little town, over the words written into the boulders with their ancient raindrops winking in the water. I reached for the ring on my chest and came up with nothing, again, and thought about what I might drop onto another silver chain to remember the weight of this summer, the weight of that canyon, the weight of my grief—all as a way to remind myself just how light I now was.

Grandpa also looked to the river, as if the answer to all our questions was out there, cutting through the seams. And maybe he was right. Maybe all rivers have the answer. Maybe all rivers have a sense of what it means to split, to catch and release, to blame and forgive, to live a life elsewhere, only to realize that all currents must eventually come back together—that all rivers must eventually meet.

Acknowledgments

First, I'd like to thank the landscape of the West, the rivers that run through it, and every writer who has attempted to characterize it, from Norman Maclean to Annie Proulx. I am haunted by waters, and I wouldn't have it any other way.

A warm thank you to Carol J. Decker for teaching me about prosthetics and her own experience as an amputee, but most importantly for teaching me what it looks like when someone courageous faces each day unbroken, unshattered.

Thanks to Brittany, my wife, for laughing at my backcast and the way I can't seem to hold a fish long enough to get a good picture of the thing. It wouldn't be an adventure without you, B. Also, thanks to Milan and T.C. for teaching me where the good holes are, even though giving away such information is equal to blasphemy and treason.

Lisa Mangum, a miracle editor, has an eye for each line, both poetic and literal. I am indebted to her for such keen insight and attention to each sentence. Chris Schoebinger and Heidi Taylor continue to rally my spirits and remind me what a good story looks like, and what good stories can do to change the world. Thank you to Troy Butcher, Callie Hansen, and the entire team at Shadow Mountain.

Many thanks to Julie Gwinn, the best agent a writer could hope for. She really is the best.

Thanks also to Lance and Steve for helping me find the right word.

And many thanks to you for giving this story a chance.

Lastly, I'd like to thank all those who struggle each day to balance who they are with who they are expected to be—by culture, by friends, by family, by religion. Please don't think you have to be only one thing. How boring is that? Be both.